The Education of a Poker Player

Also by James McManus

FICTION

Going to the Sun

Ghost Waves

Curtains

Chin Music

Out of the Blue

POETRY

Great America

Antonio Salazar Is Dead

NONFICTION

Cowboys Full: The Story of Poker

Physical: An American Checkup

Positively Fifth Street

The Education of a Poker Player

LINKED STORIES BY

JAMES MCMANUS

AMERICAN READER SERIES, NO. 25

BOA EDITIONS, LTD. ❧ ROCHESTER, NY ❧ 2015

SS

Manufactured in the United States of America

First Edition
15 16 17 18 7 6 5 4 3 2 1

Publications by BOA Editions, Ltd.—a not-for-profit corporation under section 501 (c) (3) of the United States Internal Revenue Code—are made possible with funds from a variety of sources, including public funds from the New York State Council on the Arts, a state agency; the Literature Program of the National Endowment for the Arts; the County of Monroe, NY; the Lannan Foundation for support of the Lannan Translations Selection Series; the Mary S. Mulligan Charitable Trust; the Rochester Area Community Foundation; the Arts & Cultural Council for Greater Rochester; the Steeple-Jack Fund; the Ames-Amzalak Memorial Trust in memory of Henry Ames, Semon Amzalak and Dan Amzalak; and contributions from many individuals nationwide. See Colophon on page 248 for special individual acknowledgments.

Cover Design: Sandy Knight
Interior Design and Composition: Richard Foerster
Manufacturing: McNaughton & Gunn
BOA Logo: Mirko

Library of Congress Cataloging-in-Publication Data

McManus, James.
[Short stories. Selections]
The education of a poker player : linked stories / by James McManus. — First edition.
pages ; cm. — (American reader series ; no. 25)
ISBN 978-1-938160-85-1 (softcover: acid-free paper) — ISBN 978-1-938160-86-8 (ebook)
I. Title.
PS3563.C386A6 2015
813'.54—dc23

2015019673

BOA Editions, Ltd.
250 North Goodman Street, Suite 306
Rochester, NY 14607
www.boaeditions.org
A. Poulin, Jr., Founder (1938–1996)

Contents

Altar Boy

Every other year the Holy Ghost plants a baby seed in a married mom's tummy. Nine months later a slit opens up underneath across the bottom and the baby slides out. It's not like a zipper. It doesn't go up and down but across like a smile, all at once. It just appears when the baby is ready. A few days later it heals back together without any help from the doctor who delivered the baby. That storks deliver babies is mere superstition, of course.

The dad brings the mom and the baby home from the hospital and makes arrangements with the parish secretary for the baptism. Gramma Grace is the secretary at St. Joan of Arc, so ours always go extra smoothly. We always tip the altar boys too, not like *some* families we know. Except for when I am the altar boy. As the priest sprinkles holy water over its forehead, the baby's name becomes official and can't ever be changed. *I baptize you Brian Madden Killeen in the name of the Father and of the Son and of the Holy Ghost, Amen.*

The mom is the actual mother, of course. She carries the baby around all that time, eating for two until it grows big enough to come out and start crying. To make it stop crying she nurses it, sometimes with a bottle, sometimes with one of her breasts, which are a sin to look at unless you're her husband, or unless it's honestly by accident and only for a couple of seconds. Four or five at the most. Especially nipples, which you shouldn't even think about, ever. Just long enough to know what you're looking at and decide of your own volition to look away. The same for any girl's who is old enough, the same for any woman's unless she is old.

The main difference is, God the Father is the father of Jesus. St. Joseph was Mary's husband, but still. In all other families the mom's husband is the actual father of the baby.

"But isn't the Holy Ghost His real father," I ask Gramma, "the member of the Trinity that planted the seed?"

"They're *both* the real Father of Jesus," she says. She always dips her head when she says Jesus's name. Me too, especially when it's just us talking in her love seat by the fireplace downstairs, like now, or I'm in the sacristy with Fr. Ted or Fr. Jude. It's embarrassing to do it when your friends are around, even other altar boys, but you're supposed to do it anyway. If I forget to, I always confess it.

"Remember, it's 'member *who* planted,'" she says.

"The referent isn't the entire Trinity. For that you'd say *that* or *which*."

Even if the referent is Jesus, you don't have to dip your head, only when you say J-e-s-u-s. We covered things like that last year, in third, but when it comes to the Trinity the rules for pronouns and capitals keep changing. Luckily for me, if your grandmother works in the rectory, she sometimes knows the rules better than even the nuns do. Hard to believe, but still true. I've got Sr. Geralda this year, and if I write "member that planted" on a catechism test, she wouldn't think of marking me off. That's why I always get 100. But I still remind myself to write "who" from now on. If Sr. Geralda marks me off, Gramma will have Fr. Ted speak to her.

Gramma's fireplace can't have real fires, just three plastic logs that glow pink and yellow when she plugs them in. No kids are allowed to, because we might get electrocuted. On top of the mantel is where she keeps her favorite things: two braided palm fronds, a Hummel for each grandchild, snapshots in frames (two of me, next to Grampa Vince in his uniform), and the conch shell he brought back from Scotland. Above the mantel are matching framed pictures: blue for the B.V.M. and her lilies, red for the Sacred Heart of Jesus. The flames around His heart never faze me, but the thorns pricking droplets of blood from His throbbing blue veins kind of do. I always have to look away from them, but not the same way I look away from nipples at the pool.

Gramma moved in with us when we moved out to

Lisle from the Bronx. Sometimes she still calls me her little lamb, even though I'm nine and always ask her not to anymore. To please not to. *Please.*

"Well, okaaaay," she says, "though I don't know why a good Catholic boy wouldn't want to be called Lamb of God. If it was good enough for Jesus . . ." She likes to stop talking in the middle of sentences when you know what comes next.

"Okay, okay," I tell her, "but please not when anyone else is around." She always promises not to, but sometimes she forgets.

I feel her thumb smoothing my forehead and realize I'm now in my bed. I was daydreaming again, bedtime dreaming, even though it's way *past* my bedtime. I have to serve Mass in the morning. Sometimes the dozier I get the harder I think about things, especially stuff as important as baby seeds. I must've fallen asleep on the love seat and my dad must've carried me up to my room. That's how it happens these days, since I'm too big for Gramma to carry. I was too big for her to do it *last* year, when I weighed fifty-one. Now I weigh fifty-six. Usually I just go up the stairs by myself, or stay in my room after putting on my PJs, instead of going back down to do homework with Gramma. She likes helping me in her love seat because she can smoke there, and she can't in my room. She's the one who made up that rule, and the one who enforces it on herself. Because obviously my dad, even though it's his house, can't boss around his own mom.

"Now I lay me," she says, tucking me up to my chin. She pushes the hair off my forehead and smooches me right where the Ash Wednesday smudge goes.

"Now I lay me down to sleep, I pray the Lord my soul to keep. If I should die before I wake, I pray the Lord my soul to take. God bless Gramma Grace, Grampa Vince, Gramma Betsy, Grampa Tom, my mom, my dad, Ellen, Sheila, Kevin, Colleen, and Brian."

"Amen," we both say.

"Introibo ad altare Dei." As soon as Fr. Ted says that, I say, *"Ad Deum qui laetificat juventutem meam."* I go unto the altar of God, the God who brings joy to my youth. Fr. Ted is the I and I am the youth. It makes sense. But you don't have to know exactly what every Latin word means, just be ready with the correct response and never make the priest have to wait. If you say the wrong words, the Mass can be deemed unofficial, though only real sticklers would deem that.

The thing is, if I always do a solid job serving and learn enough Latin in the seminary and maybe get my own parish and later archdiocese, it's possible that sometime early in the third millennium A.D. I'll receive the Ring of the Fisherman after being elected the first Irish American pope. First Irish *and* first American. Priests, nuns, bishops, and even the cardinals from every Catholic country would have to kiss my *Annulus Piscatoris* and obey me, but I still wouldn't ask them to because I'd be humble and modest. That's why I'd choose to be called Pope John the XXIV, or higher if XXIV has been taken. If they *wanted* to kiss my ring, I'd let them, of course. Plus I'd only make them obey me enough to make the Church's business go smoothly.

I ring the bell three times as Fr. Ted sings, *"Sanctus, Sanctus, Sanctus."*

"Benedictus qui venit," I say.

I learned how to serve by sitting in the first row at Masses. I followed where the servers went, made diagrams, and memorized all the responses. I started out at 6:15 Low Mass, like this one, because everyone has to pay their get-up-early dues. I set my alarm for five o'clock to leave time to read through the responses again. Gramma toasts English muffins and makes sure I brush my teeth and tinkle. You have to be in the sacristy twenty minutes early, to put on your cassock and surplice. Even though I'm kind of a veteran and can even handle solo assignments, she still quizzes me while we drive to the church, and of course she attends all the Masses.

She likes telling people her eldest grandson is the youngest altar boy in the parish. It was through her intercession with Fr. Ted that I got to start early, in the middle of third instead of the beginning of fifth. She must've assured him that I was beatific enough to carry out the sacred duties. And he didn't say yes just because he needed new boys for the earliest Masses.

For two-server Masses, I like the epistle side, because you get to handle the cruets at the credence table before bringing them up to the altar. As I pour the wine over Fr. Ted's fingers, I see myself upside down in the gold. You're supposed to also pour in some water, but Fr. Ted only wants you to wave that cruet over his chalice, and of course he's the boss. Of all the things altar boys do, I like pouring the wine best, because it's the *sine qua non* of the mystery of transubstantiation.

"Suscipiat Dominus sacrificium de manibus tuis, ad laudem et gloriam nominis sui, ad utilitatem quoque nostram, totiusque Ecclesiae suae sanctae," Fr. Ted says. May the Lord accept this sacrifice at Your hands, for the praise and glory of His name, for our good and that of all His Holy Church.

"Amen."

Now that he's blessed it, the wine has changed into Jesus's blood. To our senses it still looks like wine, but they often deceive us, of course. Ditto for the wafers that are about to become the body of God's only begotten Son.

I return the cruets to the table and go back to my place, kneel down, and begin the *Confiteor.* I used to genuflect each time I passed in front of the altar, and I still smite my chest each time I say *Mea culpa.* But Fr. Ted reminded me this morning that when you're going to kneel anyway you don't have to genuflect first. Little tips like that help. If your knees hurt, you offer it up.

For Communion, altar boys get their hosts first. They have SJA stamped on one side, with a cross on the other. They're unleavened white bread, like weightless half dollars without too much taste—maybe a little vanilla, but not as crumbly or sweet as a Nilla. After Fr. Ted administers mine, I bless myself, genuflect, march to the left end of the rail, and start walking backwards ahead of him as he lays one onto the tongue of each fellow communicant. You're supposed to let it melt and not chew it, but sometimes your molars bite down by accident, which God the Son understands. I try to swallow mine extra gently, to make His trip down my esophagus as unpainful as possible.

A consecrated host is never supposed to touch the floor, ever, because it's the body of Christ and you wouldn't want Him getting stepped on or vacuumed up later by a janitor. It's not like Fr. Ted would just drop one, but you still hold the paten under each chin in case someone pulls back their tongue half a second too soon. Even a minuscule crumb on the floor would be horrible, but not quite a sin as long as it was by accident. That the host wouldn't bleed if it broke, or you chewed it too hard, is all just a part of the mystery.

Only nuns and retired people come to this Mass. Mrs. Knowles in her blue and white shawl, teenie-weenie Mr. and Mrs. Kim, Mrs. O'Brien the cougher, plus half the old nuns in the convent. Their quilted gray faces tilt up, out come their veiny purple and yellow tongues, and Fr. Ted sticks on the host. Moles, broken blood vessels, hairs in their nostrils, the works. Gramma Grace always closes her eyes, at least when it's me with the paten. She always tells people I've never let a crumb touch the floor.

St. Joan students go to the eleven o'clock every day. When you serve for that one, or for High Mass on Sunday, it's not a sin to tap your friends' throats with the paten, but it is if you slide it across their skin like a dagger. A couple of Sundays ago I tapped Laura Langan's, but completely by accident. Right on the spot where her Adam's apple would be, if she had one. She must've just inched her throat forward while sticking out her little pink tongue. She's pretty with her eyes open and maybe even prettier with them closed, though she's gonna need braces on her lowers. She didn't look at me or say anything at school the next day, which was a gigantic relief because I don't even know if I like her.

For the Blessing, Fr. Ted says, *"Dominus vobiscum,"* and I say, *"Et cum spiritu tuo."* Very friendly. The Lord be with you. And with your spirit. Not "You're damning us, Nabisco. Ed comes parting her tutu," like Timmy Broun said that one time. He's in sixth.

Near the end, especially if you have to tinkle again, the words you look forward to most are *Ite, Missa est.* Go, you are dismissed.

Deo gratias!

For the first year I hardly ever got to work the epistle side or even light the candles. I only got to extinguish them, which meant my dad or Gramma had to wait an extra five minutes after Mass. My dad said it came with the territory of being the youngest. "Third-graders tend not to have much seniority, buddy," he said.

The good news was that Jim Donohoe was usually late, so I got to light them those days, though he also made me stay after to extinguish them. When Donohoe or Jim Flynn was late they'd say their mom forgot to wake them up, but wasn't that what alarm clocks were for? You had to go to bed early enough to be worthy of serving on God's holy altar. Even nuns couldn't do it, only servers and priests, as St. Peter decreed almost two thousand years ago. The only time I was late was because Gramma's green Chevy wouldn't start and my dad was on the road with his Olds. But we got a new battery and everything was fine after that.

Gramma shares the Chevy with my mom, though the ashtray is always filled with Kent filters and my mom doesn't smoke. The seats are plaid plastic, with black, white, and green stripes. The speedometer goes up to 100, but Gramma never drives even half that. It has an eagle on the hood and almost no rust. Being a year older than me is why it sometimes doesn't start. Our dad says it doesn't appreciate Chicago winters, even though they seem about as cold as the ones in New York. Maybe one degree colder is all.

Anyway, I almost told on Donohoe for making me stay to extinguish, but I didn't want Fr. Ted or Fr. Jude to think a possible future priest was a tattler. Also because even when he isn't miffed about something, Fr. Jude likes to squeeze your neck and shoulders. Sometimes he brushes his palms around your ears in these weird little circles. Plus he likes to make you talk.

Judas flapping his liverlips, Donohoe calls it. (Some sixth-graders call Fr. Ted Fr. Cheeseburger because his name is Fr. Theodore Berger, so they're probably going to Hell.) Even weirder is when there's only one server and Fr. Jude makes you stay after for breakfast. I still remember the time we were eating cornflakes and bananas and he asked me, "So, Vincent, do you have the calling or a girlfriend?"

I was too shocked to answer, but he stared hard and waited, pressing his thumb into my biceps. "Oh, definitely the calling, Father," I finally said.

"Oh, no! No girlfriend?" His lips really did look like liver. "Why's that?"

Because no one in fourth has a girlfriend! Thank God Gramma came in then and they started talking about the fundraising drive. Some people were saying the ushers were shorting it, but she and Fr. Jude agreed that my dad never would. Shorting meant stealing. But not in two thousand years would my dad think of shorting his parish. His only job on this earth is to make his parents proud of him, even though his dad died before he was one. Because he knows Grampa Vince is looking down from Heaven at the right hand of God, and They're watching.

Grampa Vince was born in Providence in 1893. He served on the *U.S.S. Baltimore*, a minelayer that booby-trapped U-boats lurking in the North Sea. He died of a heart attack when he was only thirty-six. Uncle Don was three and my dad was seven months. Gramma was nursing him when it happened. Grampa Vince was reading the *New York Times* and drinking iced tea when he suddenly hugged himself, choking, and rolled off their green wicker sofa. He didn't have life insurance because Steinway & Sons, where he was an accountant, didn't offer it, except for the big shots. Gramma's mom had to look after the boys while Gramma went to work as a bookkeeper at the Bank of Mineola. Two months later the bank laid off half its employees because of the Depression. Only dads in charge of families kept their jobs, even though Gramma was the sole supporter of hers. They became shanty Irish until the Fordham Jesuits helped them. They let my dad and Uncle Don go to Fordham Prep and Fordham U. for no charge and hired Gramma as a secretary. That's how she got her job at St. Joan, even though it's an O.S.B. parish. My dad says Benedictines are just half a notch below the old Jebbies.

Uncle Don is married to Aunt Blair and their daughter is Ashley, who's three months and two days younger than me. They live in Manhattan, but they also have a house in Sag Harbor.

If a baby dies before it's baptized, like one of Aunt Blair's did last summer, its soul goes to Limbo. It won't feel the fires of Hell, which melt your skin and let it grow back in six minutes but only so the flames can remelt it over and over again for eternity while squads of vicious devils keep stabbing the blisters on your penis and eyeballs with pitchforks. These poor downcast souls are in agony for infinity trillions of years. Thank God the babies in Limbo don't even have to feel the stinging heat of Purgatory that cleanses you of your sins, though only of the ones you've confessed. Unbaptized babies never had a chance to commit any sins, but they still never get to see God or their loved ones in Heaven. Luckily for us, everyone in our family is baptized.

With only six kids so far, we're one of the smaller families in the parish, but our house is almost as crowded as the big families' houses because Gramma needs her own room. Everyone else has to share, except me and Ellen, the oldest. Babies in cribs stay in our parents' room. Little boys and girls sleep in trundle beds. Most families have bunk beds, but our mom says they're much much too dangerous. She's stricter than our dad on most everything. She says you could roll out of the top bunk in your sleep and land on your noggin and die. That's what happened to Brendan Moseley, though at least he flew straight up to Heaven from the operating table. If you did that from a trundle, you'd only fall fourteen or fifteen inches and land on your brother or sister. You'd wake them up, granted, but no one would need to call an ambulance, get extreme unction, or call Gramma Grace to schedule a Requiem service. She wouldn't have to call any boat boys and tell them to dust off the thuribles.

During dessert, pumpkin pie, on the Sunday before

Halloween, our dad says, "In just a few months, you're going to be blessed with another little brother or sister." All the little kids clap, cheer, or boo.

"Apparently so," says our mom, shrugging like, *What can I do?*

"Ap*parent*ly," I say. No one gets it, though everyone laughs when Ellen says, "Ever heard of overpopu*la*tion?" Except for our mom.

"Apparently *not*," Ellen says.

Our mom's like, I can't believe my ears. She's about to throw one of her fits.

"Just kidding," says Ellen. She obviously wasn't, but she doesn't want her mouth to get washed out with Lava again. "No, really. I'm happy. I am."

"That's good, deah. You should be," says Gramma. To our dad she says, "Guess what Tricky Dick said today." Even seven hours after Mass, she's still wearing her ON THE RIGHT TRACK WITH JACK button. I think she started in about politics just to change the subject, to keep Ellen from getting in trouble. And it looks like it's working. Instead of Ellen's bratty remark, they're talking about Nixon's mother's loan smear or something. "A Quaker saint who needs two hundred thousand dollars?" says Gramma. "Whose son is well known to play pokah?" She really hates Nixon. Our parents don't mind him, but of course they're still voting for Kennedy because he's the best man for the job. He showed tremendous character during the war, and now he's against godless Commies.

Not only did Ellen dodge a bullet, but when she tries on her witch costume later everyone tells her how "gaw-juss" and pretty she looks. She keeps saying *thank you, my pretty* or *thank you, I'm pretty* in her stupid Wicked Witch of the West voice. The Latin for that is *persever-ate,* I think, and probably also *obnoxius.*

I'm going as Nellie Fox again, with an eight-stick wad of spearmint instead of tobacco. When I show my dad Nellie's stance—choking up lefty, right foot pointed toward third—all he says is, "Who's got the mumps?"

My mom says, "Don't you be chewing that two nights in a row now. Haven't we already got enough cavities around here?"

After spitting the wad into the garbage, I follow Gramma downstairs. I need to ask her about my own baby seed. Ever since my dad said my mom was preg-nant again, I thought it was important enough to even miss part of *Bonanza.*

"Well, Nellie, your dad is your father," she says when we get settled in, "but so is God the Father." She's old enough, all grammas are, that her breasts are called a bosom. Hers is white in between, with freckles on the tan part. It's not a sin to look at in clothes or even down into, especially when it's your gramma's.

"And the Holy Ghost too?"

She lights a fresh Kent. "Of cawse, deah."

"Because He's the one who planted the seed."

"Well, of cawse." She always says *cawse* instead of *course* and *deah* instead of *dear.* So do my mom and dad. That's how they say things back in New *Yawk.* None of us noticed the difference till we moved out to Lisle, where people think people from Boston and New York sound the same. Use your ears! Plus most of them know Senator Kennedy used to be an altar boy, but they seem to think he's only from Boston. The Kennedys of Hyannis Port, the Boston Kennedys, the Massachusetts Kennedys, etc. Gramma and I keep reminding them that when Jack was my age he was serving at St. Margaret's in the Bronx, right on 206th Street.

"They're everyone's father." The Holy Ghost and God the Father, I mean.

"Every Catholic's," she corrects me. "Only every good Roman Catholic's."

I silently repeat that so I'll remember to write it down in my catechism. I like to compare what Gramma says with what Sr. Geralda tells us in class. Plus I always put U.I.O.G.D. at the top of each page. *Ut In Omnibus Glorificetur Dei,* which means That In All Things God May Be Glorified.

"Remember what Fr. Ted tells us," says Gramma. "The Holy Ghost *helped* God the Father by planting the seed inside Mary via the Immaculate Conception."

I nod because I already knew that. *Via* in Latin means "by," and *im* means "the opposite of." *Maculate* means "stained," because *immaculate* is the opposite. *Maculations* are stains on the soul that cause birth defects and other bad things. *Conception* means "idea made flesh." It makes perfect sense. Jesus was flesh of her flesh, so Mary was exempt from all stain of original sin. In case there's any doubt, Gramma has holy cards proving it. The Holy Ghost rains down on Mary, but the Holy Ghost isn't a rain cloud. It's a white dove glowing in a bright golden light above the Blessed Virgin, or sometimes just the light beams and no B.V.M. Light beams rain down on her immaculate heart, just like the holy cards show. Most moms and girls keep them as bookmarks in their missals or purses. Most grammas too, and of course all the nuns. But how many kids do nuns have? They have none.

"You already knew that, deah, didn't you?"

"Of course," I say. "I mean, of cawse."

She lights another Kent and pretends like she's pushing me away, like I'm just too smart for her any more. I also know of at least three St. Vincents, not just De Paul. Grampa Vince and I were named for the Jesuit scholar whose relics are mostly in Ireland. He wasn't an apostle, granted, but was thought to be as pious as any of them, even though he doesn't have a feast day or holy card yet. Gramma always reminds me that Judas was Jesus's favorite apostle till he betrayed Him with a kiss for forty pieces of silver, about a hundred bucks, so sometimes being an apostle isn't all it's cracked up to be.

"So what about Mary my mom, and my dad?"

"What about them?"

"What about *my* baby seed?"

"Well, that was a seed for the ages. And now here you are, all grown up."

"But not com*plete*ly till I'm twenty-one, right?"

"Well, compared to your seed . . ." She pinches two fingers together, spreads out her arms to show me how big I am now, and taps her Kent into the ashtray.

"But who made the seed? Or like, you know, who chose it? If my dad—"

"Well, deah, your parents love each other very very much, and your dad is one of the most important young men in the parish. He's leading the drive to get other dads to half-tithe to build a new school."

I already knew that, of course. A half-tithe is one twentieth of your salary. Anything less is an embarrassment. Two percent? *Pah*. You put it in an envelope and drop it in the collection basket on Sunday or hand it to my dad or Mr. Garramone at a smoker. It's only fair that everyone chips in, so how can they not? "C'mon, buddy!" my dad tells them. "Let's get with the *program*." He's a highly trained salesman, so he's good at this stuff. He works for Precision Steel in Franklin Park, which is six towns closer to Chicago, right by O'Hare Airport. His boss is Mr. Tinsley, who'd be happy to vouch for his integrity. More than happy. My dad doesn't steal, he *sells steel*. He hands over every last dollar and every red cent he collects to Fr. Ted, who counts it all on Monday with Gramma, who keeps the books of what they've collected and who gave how much. How much is confidential, of course. Plus they still have a long way to go. Sr. Boniface, not Sr. Bony Face, drew a chart on four sheets of white cardboard taped together along the back. You can tell she used a yardstick for the sides and a protractor for the round part at the bottom. It looks like a giant outdoor thermometer with the mercury about halfway up, not the small kind that goes up your rectum. Gramma uses Magic Marker to add a little red every week.

"But so why do I look like a cross between my parents, and sort of like Grampa Vince?"

"Because your seed got plucked by the Holy Ghost from your dad's rib, and his seed got plucked from Grampa Vince's, and *his* seed got plucked—"

"Then why doesn't my dad have, like, six scars?"

"Oh my goodness. Star servers like you should know this intuitively, deah. It's like the miracle of transubstantiation. Our senses deceive us into thinking there must be a scar from each plucking."

I nodded. "But so how does the seed get planted in the womb? I know the Holy Ghost plants it by miracle, but to our *senses* how's it work?"

"Oh my gawden of roses, deah, no one learns that until they're confirmed."

"So I have to wait all the way until *eighth?*"

"Fourteen's the age of discretion—for enlisting as a soldier in Jesus's army."

We both bow our heads. "Or a sailor in His navy, don't forget."

She hugs me with her nonsmoking arm. "Just like Grampa."

"But can't you just give me a couple of hints in the meantime?"

"No, Nellie. I'm sorry. We all have our orders, you know."

My dad and I are still Yankees and Giants fans, but we also root for the Bears and the Sox, except when they're playing the Yank. It killed us when the Sox lost to the Dodgers last season, and when the Yanks lost to Pittsburgh 10-9 in the ninth of Game 7 this year. That g.d. Bill Mazeroski!

Our new town, Lisle, is twenty-four miles west-southwest of downtown Chicago. If Jesus had guided the first French explorers to settle just a few miles north of here, like in Wheaton, Lisle would be *north* of downtown, and we would've been Cubs fans. It couldn't get any weirder than that.

Nellie and I both play second. My mitt is a Nelson Fox Wilson A2100 with a Grip-Tite pocket and Pro-Lock webbing. I'm as good as our shortstop, Gordie Halladay, on grounders, but I got Mr. Salpeter to let me play second by showing him how quick I can pivot. Gordie and I turned two once in a game against Green. We're magic up the middle, just like Nellie and Little Louie Aparicio.

Gordie goes to Schiesher because his family is Protestant. He told me they only go to "services" on Easter and Christmas, and one time they even skipped Easter!

When I asked if he was baptized, he said he didn't know, but at our next game he told me he wasn't. When I told him that meant he couldn't go to Heaven and asked if he wanted me to fix this huge problem, he spit and said, "You?"

"Any altar boy can do it. I already got two years' experience."

He spit more tobacco. His parents let him chew it, but only during practices and games or when his dad takes him hunting, and because he's an only child, so he's spoiled. "Sperience doin' what?"

"Serving at baptisms. So I know all the words."

"Ya don't hafta be baptized to git inta Heaven, ya know."

My eyebrows shot up, but I tried not to laugh. "Where'd you hear *that*?"

"My folks tole me, man. What's yer problem?"

Oh boy. It looked like my work was cut out for me. But if I wanted to become a priest and maybe make bishop some day, even pope, this was the kind of mission I'd have to take on. The Jebbies, after all, might assign me to Laos or Borneo, where if you preached the wrong thing the natives would eat your flesh raw then boil your sockets to get extra marrow. But at least your soul would fly straight from their intestines to the right hand of God, plus the Archangel Michael would smite their whole tribe. Compared to converting wild cannibals, dealing with my ornery double-play partner would be a walk in Comiskey Park.

It took me only three weeks to explain to him what a drag spending eternity in Limbo would be. I didn't use pamphlets or prayer books, just good common sense between innings. Sixty million years of not seeing God or your loved ones would only be like the first second. Not *even* a second. "We're talking about e*ter*nity, man. Just think about that." He finally agreed to let me do it, "but justa shut ya the hell up." His dad didn't want me to go baptizing nobody, he said, so we'd have to do it in secret. He told me to come over to his house the next Saturday, before our game against Orange.

He lives over on Gamble, only four houses from Schiesher. The garage door was up, and his dad's truck's engine was hanging from pulleys and chains. I had on my uniform, but I used Ellen's reddish plaid scarf as a stole. I'd told Gordie to wear a white long-sleeved shirt and a red or black tie to receive the holy sacrament, but he told me his dad didn't have any ties. A house with two guys but no ties? Worse than Laos! Anyway, we moved some tackle boxes and fishing magazines off the greasy gray couch, and I told Gordie to lie back against the arm. I made sure his hands were pressed together, fingertips pointing toward Heaven. Since we didn't have a font, I dipped my finger in a cup of tap water. I asked him to please close his eyes. When he finally did, I water-painted a crucifix onto his forehead.

"I baptize you Gordie M. Halladay in the name of the Father and of the Son and of the Holy Spirit, Amen."

"That's it?" he said, opening them.

"That's all there is to it. You will now go to Heaven when you die, if you're good for the next sixty years."

"If I'm *good*? Who's the shortstop?"

"The other kind of good." I almost said I was just as good, maybe better, on grounders and pop-ups, but altar boys are supposed to be modest.

He unbuttoned the shirt, took it off. It had smudges of grease on the back, from the couch. He had a lot of muscles, for ten. "Don't feel no different," he said.

"*Yet*. Plus your brain can't always tell what your soul knows."

He shrugged, shook his head, pulled on his Purple 11.

We beat Orange that day. No double-plays, but my first saved soul had an RBI triple, and I drove him in two pitches later with a seeing-eye single to right. I could sense God was watching. No sunbeams blasting down through the clouds, but I knew. He might not be rooting for Purple, since there were plenty of good Catholics on Orange, but maybe He'd let Mrs. Halladay have other kids now, if baptisms could reverse maculations.

I called Gordie the next day to make sure he went to Mass, like he'd promised. When he said he couldn't get a ride, I told him to just confess it and start going whenever he could. If his parents didn't want him to go, it wasn't a sin to miss, as long as he made sure to go when he was old enough to drive his own car. And not just on Easter and Christmas!

"Why didn't St. Joseph and Mary have other kids?" I

asked Gramma that night. I didn't mention the Halladays. I hadn't told her or anyone else about baptizing Gordie because you're supposed to have a secret place in your heart you share only with our Lord. "Because he wasn't really Jesus's dad?"

"St. Joseph certainly *helped*," she said, "but only after Jesus was born."

"But even before that he found the manger in Bethlehem just in time, right? Because the baby slit was opening. Then provided for Mary and Jesus and taught Him how to carpent."

After blowing her smoke up away from my face, Gramma planted a big lipstick kiss on my forehead. "Baby Jesus grew up and died for our sins," she said, "then ascended unto Heaven in order to provide for each new child born into good Catholic families." Etc., etc.

She didn't want to talk about baby seeds, I guess, so I said good night and went up to my room, wiping the kiss away with my sleeve. The usual pattern was girl-boy-girl-boy-girl-boy, I knew, but sometimes it varied because of a maculation. Sr. Geralda was teaching us that maculations are caused by sins committed by a parent or grandparent. They could break the pattern or cause even worse things to happen. But she never said anything about whether baptizing a ten-year-old could *reverse* a maculation, probably because most of them worked in the other direction, from parents to kids.

I also knew babies could die before they slid out, and not just in poor countries either. They could come out deformed. Some Protestants blamed it on Thalidomide, as if God couldn't make babies' arms come out too short by Himself, as penance for huge maculations. Even one sin against His Word, even a venial, could alter the pattern or cause other defects. Sins of concupiscence were the most common causes by far. Looking at pictures in *Playboy* could do it, of course. Geralda never actually said that, I just figured it out by myself. Ogling breasts or peeking up a skirt could *easily* cause one, or even a bare ankle in the olden days under Queen Victoria, around when Gramma and Geralda were born. Plus even if concupiscent thoughts weren't sins, they tempted you to commit impure acts. That's how concupiscence of the eyes led to concupiscence of the flesh, making venials explode into mortals. Breasts, fannies, thighs, or even pretty faces could be sparks that ignited dry tinder.

People might ask, whyever would you look at a thigh or a fanny? Because the Devil always tempts you to, while your guardian angel helps you resist. But it's not like a red guy with little red horns sits on one shoulder and a white guy with a gold halo sits on the other, with each one yelling orders into one of your ears. That's mere superstition. In the first place, most devils and angels are invisible. In the second place, they're both small enough to fit inside your heart and your brain at the same time, encouraging you to look and not look.

Sometimes you couldn't help listening to a devil, no matter how hard you prayed, just like some adults couldn't help being drinkers. Uncle Don was turning *into* one, even though he was still a good Catholic. That's why my cousin had died that summer, before it was baptized or even slid through the slit. Uncle Don had his grouchy look when we visited them in Sag Harbor. Ashley was as tall as me and had extra freckles, but she didn't seem sad. She was normal, which meant she played with Ellen, not me, though we all dove through breakers and combed for petrified sharks' teeth at the beach. Aunt Blair stayed upstairs or out in the sun room. Uncle Don didn't want to talk about Limbo. He didn't even say, Let's not talk about that. He just sort of ignored me when I asked him about it.

He and my dad drank martinis. Uncle Don called them martins. "Another mahtin, Kev?" He drank at least twice as many, my mom said. She was eating for two that summer, with Brian inside her. Uncle Don was drinking for two.

The dead baby was probably a boy, I figured, because Ashley was a girl. The maculation must've been huge, because it caused her almost-brother to die but didn't change it back to a second girl seed in a row, like a smaller one might've. The Holy Ghost made girl and boy seeds in a way so they couldn't be switched.

Gramma didn't want to talk about it either. Not in her love seat or while driving to church. Not ever, I guess. Our mom did, on the phone to Miss Kerry, but not when our dad was around. Or else they just whispered about it in bed. I heard them sometimes from the hall, but not every word. Our mom wasn't a fan of Uncle Don *or* Aunt Blair. Uncle Don was vice president of British Aluminum, and he got lots of perks. Aunt Blair had grown quite accustomed to them. My mom also said they spent money like it was going out of style. "Like it grows on trees and they own the g.d. forest. Everything has to be oh so posh."

I'd have to be older, probably not till Confirmation, to know if perks or poshness added up to a fatal maculation, or getting drunk all the time was enough by itself. Ellen hadn't been confirmed yet, but even if she already knew, she probably wouldn't tell me, though she really liked being a know-it-all. So I had to figure out a lot of these things by myself.

Like the Shurbas, who lived over on Jonquil. They had, no joke, seven straight girls before Tommy was born, and only God knew what maculations had caused it. Mrs. Shurba once told my mom, "We make lotsa button holes," but what the heck was that supposed to mean? In our family the girl-boy pattern was holding steady, unless this one after Brian comes out with a penis. Anything was possible, because nobody's family, except for maybe the Kennedys, was perfect.

"So what could the sin've been," I asked Gramma, "to cause the girl-girl-girl-girl-girl-girl-girl?" This was after we got back from Long Island, but I wasn't asking about Aunt Blair's baby, only about the Shurbas' weird pattern.

"Some things are not for us to know, Vince," she

said. She always sniffed in this funny way when she didn't want to talk about something, tilting her chin down a little. "Pushing to understand every last thing is why Eve and Adam got expelled from the Garden of Eden. Seven girls or two boys in a row were just part of God's plan, like Uncle Don and your dad. We're happy for the family we have." Though sometimes she didn't look happy.

"Could it've been because Uncle Don is a drinker?" I couldn't help asking that because I'd heard my mom say he was a terrible drinker. An alkie, she called him one time. My dad said it too, about his own brother, so it must've been true.

"No, Vince, it couldn't. I don't know where you heard that."

"No, nowhere, you're right. It couldn't've."

"Jesus provides for every child the Holy Ghost helps to be born." Sniff. Chin down. Sniff. "Boy *or* girl. *Whatever* the parents have done."

That was that.

On Sundays when it's cold out, Gramma wears her stole of three foxes. Two of their mouths are clamped to the one in front of it, just above the tail. They hang across her shoulders and drape down the front, with the fox on her right facing down and the one on her left facing up, unless she has them wrapped around her neck. Their eyes are reddish brown glass, but everything else is real fox: ears, legs, and tails, even all twelve of their little paws, with five creepy black fingers each.

She loves her fox stole because her sons gave it to her for her fiftieth birthday, but it isn't her favorite thing. Her favorite thing is the conch shell Grampa Vince brought back from Scapa Flow. Pale glossy pink on the inside, maybe six inches high, with forty-two spines, like hard nipples, spiraling up to its tip. Gramma says when you press the open side to your ear, you can hear the North Sea, where he laid mines to blast the Hun U-boats. "He brought it home just for me, even though when he found it we still hadn't met."

When I asked her how that worked, she said, "The Creator of the Universe works in mysterious ways. That's why Grampa died when he was only thirty-six, and why you were born, deah, to live out the rest of his days."

A few weeks later the weirdest thing happened. Tom Zrout, a sixth-grader, told me it was the circulation of your blood you heard inside seashells. We're walking up Riedy Road and he's talking about a vacation his family took to Florida, his sisters went beachcombing, etc., so I told him about Gramma's shell.

"That's b.s.," he said. Just like that. He still had a tan from their trip, but his big nose was peeling. "How can you hear the North Sea from God-damn Lisle, Illinois? Are its waves like a million feet high?"

And get this—Zrout is an altar boy! I'd just served with him a couple of weeks ago. "My gramma says the shell carries the sound inside it forever," I said. "She ain't a b.s.-er, believe me."

"Forever, huh? Just stays in there for like a million centuries?"

"Even more. Way way way *way* more. For an infinite number."

"And none of it leaks out or anything?"

"So you're saying sound 'leaks'?"

"Jesus Christ!" He looked like he wanted to slug me. "I guess if your *gramma* told you, it's *gotta* be true." He cackled like a hen, or a monkey. "Fuck you very much for explaining that."

Swearing was a sin, but the weirdest thing about it was that some fairly good Catholics still did it. Some way better Catholics than Zrout was.

My dad, for example. Every week he drives to places like St. Louis and Bettendorf, or flies to Detroit or Paducah. He leaves on Monday or even Sunday night and sometimes won't get home till Friday. He gets a salary plus commission. The more orders he gets, the more money he makes, but only after he does his expenses. The God-damned expenses, he calls them when his mom isn't listening.

Our mom knows he swears sometimes, but she doesn't say anything about it, at least not in front of us. Men swear, it's a sin, and that's that. When he's tired or grouchy, Gramma tells me, He's unda a lotta presha, deah. She says his main concern is making sure we have a nice house and enough to eat because *he* never had that. Even though Jesus always provides for good Catholic families, dads still have to work long and hard, with God and man working together for the benefit of all wives and children. If Catholic men swear, confess it, and make sincere acts of contrition, God forgives them. But if they swear or drink and confess it but don't stop swearing or drinking, they're probably going to Hell. It's not for us to know definitely, but you can still figure out what will probably happen. I just hope my dad will know what to do.

In fifth I start reading about President Kennedy. "Here is the man who's made us so proud," Gramma tells me, showing me one of the articles she saves in her closet. Every week he's in *Life* or *Time*, sometimes both. His hair is always dry, not slicked back like most dads'. And short sideburns. His official picture—pinstripe suit, tie slightly crooked—is in a Kelly green frame next to our dining-room thermostat. The day Gramma hung it, I decided to use much less Brylcreem.

Just like the Killeens and the Maddens, the Kennedys lived in the Bronx for a while, when Jack was in fifth and sixth. Gramma even saw him there once. His family belonged to St. Margaret of Cortona Parish on West 206th Street.

"A woman's the patron saint of our parish too," Ellen says during dinner, even though *I* brought it up.

"That's right, deah," says Gramma.

"Also a martyr," says Ellen. "St. Joan was called the Maid of Orléans because she never got married, not because she cleaned up." She adds that detail so the little kids can follow along. "She was a warrior who led us in the Hundred Years' War. A Protestant general tried to dishonor her, but she fought him off and preserved her chastity. She cut her hair short and wore men's clothes to keep other Protestants from besmirching her maidenhead. But because she led Catholics against them, they burned her alive as a heretic in 1431, when she was nineteen. It was they who were the heretics though. The Protestant who lit the fire, Geoffroy Thérage, was condemned to the lowest circle of Hell, not far above Judas."

"Very well done," says our mom. Our dad says, *"Bravo! Bravissimo!"*

But Ellen only knows all this because she had to write an essay about it. Sr. Bonita gave her the only A+ in the class.

"So what kind of name's *Geoffroy Thérage* supposed to be, anyway?" I ask.

Almost everyone laughs, plus when Kevin repeats the name, the adults boo and hiss. But when Ellen rolls her eyes and says, "Protestant, obviously," our dad and Gramma laugh even louder.

I decide to write an essay about President Kennedy. I'll read and listen and watch the news and take tons of notes to make sure it's better than Ellen's. Not better for a fifth-grader either. Better, period.

The Kennedys lived at 232nd Street and Independence Avenue. It was the grandest mansion in the Riverdale section of the Bronx, which had many large houses with nursemaids and regular maids—the kind that cleaned up. The president's father was a successful enough businessman to be named ambassador to England. He didn't hate Jews, my dad says, though he wasn't the world's biggest fan of them. He didn't like Hitler either. Gramma says he was so opposed to alcohol he gave each of his sons a thousand dollars not to drink it. His daughters got two thousand. But it was their mother, Rose Fitzgerald Kennedy, who really put the starch in their Catholic backbone. She'd attended the Convent of the Sacred Heart, so the most important thing in the world to her was for her sons to serve on God's altar. Back in the nineteenth century her husband had been an altar boy at Our Lady of the Assumption in Boston, but it was Rose who spoke to the pastor at St. Margaret's, Msgr. Joseph Doyle, to make sure her sons got to serve, just like Gramma did for me. Rose informed him that Jack was an altar boy at St. Aidan's in Brookline, Massachusetts, before they moved to the Bronx. That was all Msgr. Doyle needed to hear. He made Jack a St. Margaret's altar boy that very morning. His brothers Joe, Bobby, and Teddy served too. Many parishioners believed Bobby was the most talented, passionate server, with Jack as runner-up in that department. Gramma said there wasn't any shame in this though, because serving on God's altar was not a competition.

When he grew up and was ready to start a family, Jack was married to Jacqueline Bouvier by Archbishop Cushing. They now have two kids, a girl then a boy, same as our pattern. Caroline was born in '57, like Sheila, and John John is about the same age as Brian. 'Twas a grand thing for Catholics and the country that members of the One True Church finally got to live in the White House. "All those long years of prejudice are ovah, buddy," my dad says. "Done. Adios."

Gramma agrees. She says Jack was the first president to serve on the altar *and* in the navy. He was elected because he was the best man for the job, period. No responsible voter believed the Southerners who said he wanted to replace the gold in Fort Knox with consecrated hosts or to kiss the Pope's ruby slipper. He wasn't a pretty boy either. He was a Harvard man and a war hero. "Don't get me wrong, deah. President Eisenhower was a good man and a staunch anti-Communist, but President Kennedy, well . . ." She didn't have to say any more.

Another time she said to my dad, "The Kennedy men aren't gamblers, deah. They're too busy working for the good of the country." We were driving to confession on Saturday morning, after one of the Friday night smokers. Gramma said she'd found out that some of the dads had played poker in the St. Joan church basement. "Until two fifteen in the mawning!" she said. My dad had been at the smoker but of course hadn't played. "My Gawd," Gramma said. "Bobby and Jack don't smoke or drink either." My dad just kept driving and nodding and smoking. Gramma wasn't mad at him though, because she was smoking too. She was just making a point about how "unseemly" it is to gamble and drink. "Ike and Dick almost never *stopped* playing poker," she said. When my dad said, "There was a war on, ya know," she said, "As if *that's* an excuse."

I read that all the Kennedys were navy men, just like my dad, Uncle Don, Grampa Vince, and Uncle Thomas. Grampa Tom and his father had both worked in the Brooklyn Naval Yard, which was just as important as serving on a dreadnought or an Essex-class carrier. If there's ever another war, I'll join the navy too, either as a sailor or a chaplain. Both are exactly as honorable because every man comes under fire in wartime. Hun U-boats, Cuban guerrillas in stolen yachts, and Jap kamikazes in Zeros killed chaplains just as dead as any other sailor. They sent them forty fathoms below, which got them up to Heaven the quicker.

The next war will probably be with Cuba, Russia, and China. Castro, Khrushchev, and Mao are godless bastards and the Iron Curtain a disgrace of pure evil. My dad says we might have to bomb the daylights out of them someday to save their people from those atheist dictators, especially if Khrushchev builds a wall in Berlin. Plus they can't keep cheating at the Olympics and expect to get away with it. Look at how all their best people are trying to escape from no freedom of religion. We cannot sit by on our fannies. As President Kennedy said, "Ask not what your country can do for you, ask what you can do for your country."

The president is a war hero because he served as commander of the *PT-109*. PT stands for Patrol Torpedo, which we needed because the Japs used sneak torpedo attacks all over the Pacific, not just at Pearl Harbor. On August 2, 1943, the *109* was cut in two by the Jap destroyer *Amagiri*. Lt. Kennedy commanded his men to swim six miles to Plum Pudding Island, then to Olasana Island. He had to tow one of the wounded by a rope between his teeth, which gave him a bad back, which was why he needed a rocking chair in the Oval Office. He and his crew survived for six days by drinking coconut milk. It was Lt. Kennedy's idea to send an S.O.S. by carving their location inside a coconut shell. "*Waste not want not* must've been his motto," says Gramma.

For my eleventh birthday I got a *PT-109* model kit. I already had the glue and the paint, but it took me five days to assemble because it was Skill Level 2. It had four crewmen and was powered by three twelve-cylinder Packard engines. Four torpedo tubes, four 20mm machine guns, one antiaircraft gun. I painted the tubes black and the guns gray, then glued on little strips of paper painted red and yellow to look like fire blasting out. The smell of glue and paint made me woozy, which I thought was how martinis made you feel, so I swore for about the eightieth time to not become a drinker.

If only I got a thousand bucks for not doing it! Even after half-tithing, it'd be enough to buy a used Chevy with whitewalls and FM by the time I turned sixteen.

The Revell and Lindberg catalogs didn't show kits for the *Baltimore.* Fat Stan at the Hobby Shop said they'd never carried it, but if he came across one he'd send me a postcard. The only kits for ships built before the twentieth century were for the *Monitor* and the *Merrimack*. He said it was funny because just a couple days ago someone *else* came in asking about a *Baltimore* kit.

"Was it a woman who tawked like this? Reddish hair, about this tall?" I put out my hand about an inch above the top of my head.

"Yep, that's her." Everyone said Stan was retarded, but he was a decent guy and actually pretty smart, at least about models and stuff.

The card with the *109* kit had said "From: Mom and Dad," but Gramma must've helped pick it out. The present officially from her was Grampa Vince's mitt from when he played second for the *Baltimore* when they played teams from other ships in the Yankee Mining Squadron. My dad said she'd been saving it for him, then for me, in her cedar chest, ever since he went off to the navy in '46. It was brown and stiff and small, almost flat. He said mitts like that worked because back in the dead-ball era baseballs were softer. Mitts like my A2100 weren't invented yet, so you had to be a way better fielder back then. Two hands, bend your knees, and all that.

My dad wasn't going to cry, but I could tell he was sad because he'd never played catch with his dad. Gramma did cry, of cawse, because she missed Grampa Vince. She told me after dinner that they didn't get married until 1923. By then he had his job as an accountant at Steinway & Sons in Astoria. They'd met in June of 1922. She was a bookkeeper living with her mother and sister in Greenwich Village. They fell in love and got engaged and got married on August 25, 1923, at St. Joseph's Church on Waverly Place. They bought a house in Carl Place, nine miles east of the Steinway plant. She was twenty-five, he was thirty. Uncle Don was born eleven months later, and my dad was born October 20, 1927, the year Ruth hit sixty.

On June 20, 1928, Grampa Vince had a heart attack on the porch of their house. He died the next morning, so my dad never got to talk to him. Almost right away, they were poor. My dad says even though movies cost only two cents when he was a kid, he and his brother sometimes couldn't come up with four cents to go see one. (He usually says this when he's talking about the "scads" of loose change on top of our dryer or in between the couch cushions.) "But your grandmother kept us afloat. She also made sure my father's Jesuit values were taken to heart by his sons." Then he kissed Gramma Grace, who started bawling all over again.

A couple days later, Gramma told me that if any member of a family was ordained, every member of his family received a dispensation from Purgatory. When they died they'd go directly to Heaven. I knew this already, but I acted surprised. "Under Diocesan law," she said, "it's a plenary indulgence," showing me the parts she had underlined in a book: *his family shall receive the extra-sacramental remission of a temporal punishment due to be served in Purgatory.*

The way it worked, she said, was that God forgave all of a priest's family's sins, so no one had to spend time in Purgatory. Forgiveness was granted via the Promise of the Keys. "Most indulgences remove only part of the punishment," she said, "but a plenary indulgence, such as an ordination, removes *all* of it."

Purgatory was where sins were purged by fires that glowed against your skin but didn't blister or melt you, like Hell's fires did. For a medium-sized family's total, we were talking about millions of years getting singed. Priests' families all got to skip that, except for his in-laws. That's why Gramma, who'd committed hardly *any* sins and whose brothers-in-law were both priests, would still have to get stung in Purgatory. She could only be spared that if I became a priest before she died, which could happen any day to a gramma.

"I'm gonna do it ASAP then," I said.

"Oh, deah, I'm just so . . . Are you shuah?"

"I've wanted to do it ever since third, but now it's official." Plus Ellen couldn't save her. No way. "I love you so much, Gramma," I said.

When she finally let me go from an extra-tight hug,

we mapped out my path to ordination. We drew arrows from altar boy (1958–1964) to seminarian (1965–1972) to priest (1972–20??). I'd keep serving at St. Joan but enroll in a Jesuit seminary for high school. Then the rectors would send me to a university. Maybe Fordham, maybe Notre Dame, maybe St. John's or Holy Cross. Maybe Georgetown. Just like my dad's were, all my expenses for high school and college would be paid by the Society of Jesus. As soon as I graduated, I'd receive Holy Orders and the dispensations would kick in automatically.

Before we mapped out the plan, I'd assumed I'd go to St. Procopius, out past the DuPage River toward Naperville. There was really only one hill in Lisle, and Proco was at the top of it. The teachers were mostly Benedictines, and almost every St. Joaner went there. If you didn't it meant your parents had lapsed in their faith. Lisle High was right behind our backyard, and I'd been playing baseball on its diamonds since we moved in, but of course I could never go there.

When I told Gramma again how much I wanted to do it, she said, "But let's not tell Mom and Dad yet. Let's have it be a surprise."

A week later a brochure from St. Stanislaus Seminary in Florissant, Missouri, was sitting in the middle of my desk, with a note in Gramma's cursive: *It came!*

The brochure said the place was like a medieval monastery. Its 999 acres had an orchard, a cattle barn, wheat fields, vineyards, an abattoir, and a bakery. I scanned every page for a baseball diamond, but none was mentioned or pictured. And why not just get one more acre? The chalices dated to the 1650s and were used in ministries throughout the Midwest. Some orders had monasteries, but the Jebbies, who were smarter, had ministries.

I slid the brochure between some *Sports Illustrateds* in my magazine drawer. To hide something big from your parents wasn't a sin of omission if it was one of *their* parent's idea to give the middle parents a happy surprise. But keeping four pages from Gramma's Spiegel catalog's Maidenform section were definitely sins of commission *and* omission: commission by tearing them out, omission by not asking her, commission by looking at them while impurely touching oneself, major omission for failing to confess it. Added all up, it might even be my first mortal. St. Augustine says it depends on the frequency of the i.t.o.'s, though he doesn't give the minimum number. Each i.t.o. is a venial or mortal depending on whether it's a "morose delectation." Sr. Francona hasn't covered that term yet, and I obviously can't ask my parents or Gramma.

I kept those four pages inside the January 16 *SI* with Cousy on the cover. (My dad doesn't follow pro basketball, so he'd never think to borrow it.) After hiding the brochure, I pulled out those pages, folded them three extra times, slid them into my pocket, and took them across the hall to the bathroom. I was trying so hard not to have an i.t.o., and to avoid getting caught with the tinder, I was shaking from my knees to my jaw. I locked the door, glanced in the mirror to see how guilty I looked—as Judas Iscariot with dirty blond hair and pimples on his chin—and tore the sheets into small enough pieces to flush down in one try. I scanned the counter and floor to see if any telltale shreds had popped loose. None had, but I flushed it again to make sure.

That night I had a hideous dream about flushing the toilet. One piece showing these really nice breasts in a lacy black Chansonette bra kept swirling back up. No matter how often I jiggled the handle, it would not effing flush. It was taking like forty-five minutes for the tank to fill up. When I finally got the top off, I saw that the chain between the valve and the float ball was broken again. Then the bathroom was crowded with priests and parishioners, who could all see the cleavage, even though the wet shred was smaller than a piece of g.d. confetti!

In the morning I realized I'd had another wet dream, though everything in the nightmare had been the exact polar opposite of concupiscent. Having to clean up my sheet and underpants and mix them down to the bottom of my hamper before anyone knocked or barged in made me decide being celibate would make everything much much much easier. So the plan to go to St. Stanislaus was perfect for that reason too.

I didn't say anything about it as Gramma drove us to 6:15 Mass, but I knew she could tell I was psyched.

Concupiscence

About the only time Ellen and I walked to school together since I was in second and she was in fourth, she asked me if I knew Mrs. Kennedy had a stillborn kid before Caroline. I shook my head, nodded. Stillborn meant still, as in not moving because it was dead, not still being born. It could've died a few days before but not months before because then it would've stopped growing and people would see the mom's stomach not getting bigger. I think it was also called a macular discharge, but I didn't say that to Ellen. The only reason we were walking together was I had to help carry part of her seventh-grade project about Abraham Lincoln to school. She had the wooden base with the facts and dates lacquered on, and I had the papier mâché head. She'd painted it the color of a shiny new penny, and the paint wasn't even all dry yet.

"Maybe *two* babies," she said. She was wearing one of her sweaters that showed she had breasts, though our mom always tried to make sure her maroon blazer covered them up. It was weird to have a sister who had them. "Plus she needed cesareans for John John *and* Caroline."

She was watching to see if I knew what that meant. I pretended to adjust my grip on the stupid head so I wouldn't have to say anything. Just because his head was on the penny didn't mean his face was the color of one, plus his hair should've been brown, not shiny bronze-pink! Finally she said, "The doctor had to slice open her womb with a scalpel and pull out the baby."

What? "But wouldn't that kill the First Lady? I mean, before she became—"

"Not if he does it extremely carefully and sews you back up right away."

To mock her I snorted and said, "Like sews it with a needle and *thread?*"

"With sutures and stitches, you dunce. Anesthetics too, if there's time. They take the stitches out later, but you still have a scar."

"And it doesn't go away after—after the baby comes out?"

She looked at me like I was the stupid one. "That's why they call it a scar?"

"Oh, yeah, is *that* why?"

"It's named after Julius Caesar," she said. "His mother was one of the first ones who got cut open like that. And she died! The Roman doctors hadn't learned how to sew moms back up yet."

Then it got even weirder. As we turned the corner at Riedy and Columbia, she said, "That's why I'm not having babies even *after* I get married."

"Wha'd'ya mean, even after?"

"Not then and not ever."

"But it happens to moms automatically."

"Not every *time*. Not when God knows she doesn't want it to."

I almost asked how God could know that, before I remembered omniscience. But that didn't mean He had to agree to everything every married woman wanted or didn't want. God didn't *have* to do anything. But even if it happened automatically, being omnipotent could also let Him *keep* a baby seed from being planted. Mrs. Mays didn't have any kids, and neither did Mrs. Mahaffey. Did that mean they had maculations or that they just didn't want to?

As the guard at Division was crossing us, Ellen said, "Not if I used the rhythm method."

The guard, Mr. Kim, gave Ellen a look. All I could say was, "Yeah, right."

She slowed down and glared, like *Don't talk back to seventh-graders, sonny.* I started walking faster. "Yeah, right?" she said, catching up. "Yeah right *what*?"

Dale Peters, a sixth-grader, was in front of us now, so I lowered my voice. "But so what could cause *two* maculations in a family as good as the Kennedys?"

She not only laughed at me, but easily loud enough for Peters to hear. "I guess that's not for us to know, sonny boy." She was so sarcastic it made me want to smash Lincoln's head on the sidewalk. I might've even done it if we weren't in front of the school now, with a nun spying out every window. Plus I knew she'd tell on me, especially if she flunked because her project got pulverized.

I carried it up to her classroom but didn't say you're welcome when she thanked me. It was the first time I'd been in 208, the room for the smart seventh-graders. The boys were so g.d. tall. The bell was about to ring, but most of them were still standing around talking or setting up their projects. One was a painting of Pope John XXIII that made him look like Jimmy Durante. The biggest was a basketball covered in tinfoil held up by four metal fishing rods with the guides and handles cut off. *Sputnik 1.* Good luck on your next family fishing trip!

Ellen wasn't, but some of the other girls were even taller than the boys. A couple of them had these massive boobs in their sweaters, like Notre Dame cheerleaders. Ellen's desk was next to Dory Yackley's, whose weren't that big. People called her a little number because the rest of her looked like a movie star, except she wasn't that tall. Her project was a heart-shaped red box and a parchment scroll rolled in from both ends and tied with a black satin bow. It was supposed to be about something from history, but I couldn't tell how they went together.

"So who's your helpful little helper?" she said.

"Oh, no one," said Ellen. But then she gave in. "Vince, you know Dory."

I nodded and said hi. She said hi too. I tried to move past her, but she stood in front of me and mussed up my hair. She smelled sort of like coconut frosting.

"What's this, Vince, the dry look?"

"The bell!" I said, grazing her elbow and skirt as I ducked past her, heading for the door. I could still hear her laughing as I ran back downstairs to my locker. I clipped on my SJA tie and made it to my seat with maybe a second to spare—and pink paint on my tie and fingers and the bell buzzing fifty times louder than usual.

If I asked Gramma Grace about Mrs. Kennedy's stillbirths, I knew she'd tell me ours is not to know the reason why. If my mom wasn't listening, my dad would say something like "Jackie's a gorgeous gal and all, but do we have to listen to that *voice* of hers for the next six years? Jeeezus."

I decided to ask Fr. Ted, but the next few times I was with him in the sacristy we were always running late before Mass. I couldn't ask during confession because you were there to confess your own sins, not ask him about other people's. Even if I did ask, he'd probably say something about the sanctity of the confessional and ask why I wanted to know.

One Friday night I heard my dad mention Joe Kennedy, the president's dad. He and Mr. Hudson were talking politics. After I brought them a new tray of cubes, I stayed close to listen. Mr. Hudson was for Nixon, but he and my dad were still friends. My dad admitted Nixon might've even handled the steel crisis better than the president was. Mr. Hudson wasn't in steel, but he didn't like what the president said about the prices. "What's the guy know about bidness?" he said.

My dad said, "The old man taught him all he needs to know."

"He teach him to attack free enterprise? Attack U.S. Steel, for Chri-sake?" I think he saw me standing by the refrigerator, because he lowered his voice as he said something else. About an actress, I think.

My dad said, "Maybe the old man ain't the best Catholic around, but—"

"Or going soft on the Nazis? The hell was that all about?"

Maybe what'd happened with U.S. Steel and the Nazis had caused maculations in his two almost-grandchildren. I wanted to ask them about it when my dad said, "Well, Huddie, I'll tell you what was going on as soon as Vince here heads upstairs to do his homework."

"I only have eight math problems left. I got all day tomorrow and Sunday."

"Yeah, but now's a great time to get started."

As I headed upstairs, Mr. Hudson called, "What's the cube root of twenty-seven?"

I shouted back "three" and kept going.

He and my dad started hooting, and Mr. Hudson shouted, "What about the cube root of pi?"

Screw you, Mr. Hudson, I thought.

I didn't confess that because I didn't say it, just thought it. When I confessed to Fr. Jude about looking at Dory and Laura, I found out it wasn't a sin to look at girls' faces but maybe it was to look at the backs of their knees. When he said, "Tell me more," I whispered through the screen, "Between the bottom of their skirt and the top of their socks."

"Speak up, my son. Fronts or backs?"

"Both. Mostly backs, though. I was sitting behind her at Mass and—"

"Whose? Behind whom?"

"The Langans, Father. Laura's."

"Ah, yes, Miss Langan's. I see." He thought for a while. "The backs of boys' knees and girls' knees look much the same to us, yes?" They didn't, but I didn't say anything. "And we see boys' knees and legs, all their parts, in outline at least, on the playing fields and courts. Noticing such things is natural, not even a venial sin as long as you have no impure thoughts *with respect to* the knees, buttocks, shoulders, and so forth. You simply mustn't do anything Jesus Himself wouldn't do if *He* saw them. Even if it wasn't, as you say, by accident. And girls like Miss Langan and Miss Yackley have a responsibility to perhaps dress more modestly."

I was afraid to say it wasn't their fault, so I just said, "Yes, Father."

My penance for fibbing, teasing siblings, etc., came

to only three Hail Marys and six Our Fathers, which I said walking home instead of in the pew. I was sorry but glad I hadn't confessed to tapping throats with the paten. Kneeling and talking about all those knees made my knees hurt and gave me a boner when I passed Laura's house, though it wasn't her fault that her knees were so perfect. Uniforms were uniforms. Her knee-socks always came to exactly the right place, not too high, not too low. Picture perfect. The hem of her skirt might've been a smidgen too high for Sr. Regina, but not high enough to be sinful, or sinful to look at.

I touched myself impurely that night. And almost every night after that, sometimes twice or three times, usually into a sock. Sometimes dirties, sometimes clean ones when the dirties ran out. I usually thought about Laura first, then Dory or a real movie star. Sometimes in blouses, sometimes in sweaters, knee-socks and skirts always perfect.

The g.d. i.t o.'s were definitely getting the best of me.

The Langans lived at the corner of Gamble and Center, two thirds of the way between school and my house. When Laura and I happened to walk home at the same time, I could speed up or slow down to make sure I'd wind up right next to her. She usually walked with Donna Lehigh or Angie Barotka, but sometimes by herself. One time a snowflake landed on one of her long curved blond eyelashes. I almost reached out to touch it, God knows why, but she blinked it off before I did anything stupid. She had great knees and legs because she did gymnastics at some place called Sokol. I'd ask her how Sokol was going and she always said, "Fine." Her picture in the yearbook, the one with her hair in a flip, always gave me a boner, just from her hair, neck, and face.

It even worked with Angie's sometimes.

For Memorial Day, Fr. Ted came over for dinner. Even though he ate with us two or three times a year, the only higher honor would be if a cardinal or President Kennedy came over. (Pope John didn't count. He was too busy to ever leave the Vatican that long with his retinue.)

Fr. Ted looked skinnier in his regular clothes than he did in his vestments, and of course was less solemn—more like he was in the sacristy than up on the altar. When my dad asked him if he wanted the usual, he said, "I think I'm going brown tonight, Kev." That meant a Manhattan, which was named after where I was born, in St. Elizabeth's Hospital. The only other thing I'd seen him drink was altar wine, which didn't count because after I poured it over his fingers and he consecrated it, it was the Blood of the Lamb and couldn't get you drunk anymore. The weirdest coincidence was, we were having lamb that night too, with mint jelly, corn, and mashed potatoes. To be extra good hosts, my dad and Gramma also went brown, and my mom had a Coke instead of a 7-Up. After clinking glasses, they looked at the fund-raising numbers, nodding and pointing and whispering.

After my dad made him another Manhattan, Fr. Ted sat down next to me on the couch. Ellen was still upstairs and the younger kids were running around crazy, as usual. My mom had Brian and my dad was trying to get the others to come to the table. Walter Cronkite was on, but I jumped up and lowered the sound and sat back down next to Fr. Ted. His sideburns were what you called salt and pepper, but it wasn't like he had to retire or anything.

"So, Vince." He swirled the new ice cubes around. "We still feel that call?"

"I think so, Father." I kept my voice down because Gramma was listening in from the kitchen. "But how do you know for sure? How did *you* know?"

"Well, the mystery of whether God is calling you isn't like the mystery in one of these British detective novels. He isn't cleverly trying to trick you into suspecting the wrong choice is the right one. He's too gracious for that. That's where your grandmother's name comes from, by the way. From His Grace." If Gramma heard him she'd smile, because she loved Fr. Ted. It wasn't just keeping the books and making him coffee and sandwiches. She *loved* him. Sometimes she said she adored him, even though he wasn't S.J. I realized he'd probably told me her name came from His Grace so she'd hear him and feel good. As a bonus for being his best secretary ever.

President Kennedy was saluting some admiral and Fr. Ted was saying I had a multitude of paths toward my union with God. I should remain prayerful and talk to other young people about how my faith in Jesus affected my life. Help them see that a holy, happy life involved sacrifice. I wished I had my blue spiral notebook, but I didn't worry too much because I knew I'd remember all this. After dinner I'd go up and write it down anyway, and not think at all about Laura. Or at least, if I did, without an i.t.o., especially not the same hand I shook Fr. Ted's with.

That summer was the first time I visited Grampa Tom and Gramma Betsy without my parents. I flew to LaGuardia Airport by myself, and they picked me up when we landed. I forgot my Tom Dooley book on the plane, but it was too late to run back and get it because Grampa was already putting my suitcase in the trunk. Gramma said they'd buy me another one.

"That's okay," I said. I was scrunched between them on the scratchy wool seat. It was hotter than it was in Chicago. The rosary wrapped around the rearview mirror stem was the same kind my mom had: olive wood, with tarnished silver links. "It was kind of boring. Not *that* boring, though."

"We'll get you another copy," she said. That was that, even though she didn't ask me what the title was.

"Were da stewardesses pretty?" asked Grampa.

"*Were* they! One of them's name was Laura, same

as my girlfriend."

He gave me thumbs-up. "Did she fluff up yaw pillow for ya?"

"Now that'll be quite enough about that," Gramma said. "Watch the road."

"The pillows on planes are so small," I told them, holding my hands about ten and a half inches apart.

"Mary says he's girl-crazy enough as it is," Gramma said.

Their apartment was in Parkchester, but we drove straight to Lake Mahopac. Grampa was a building inspector, and he was building a cottage up there. It had a roof and a floor but no solid walls yet. There were only about five other houses on their street, which was mostly gravel and sand. Lots and lots of trees, more than anyplace I'd ever seen. Even more than the Arboretum, though of course not as many different kinds.

We slept on army surplus cots or in hammocks hung from eye-hooks in the joists. For dinner we grilled burgers or hot dogs while their son, Uncle Thomas, drove to the gas station for more buns or ice. "Our shanty-Irish campgrounds," Gramma Betsy called it. The toilets didn't work yet, and she said it was my job to empty the slops into the woods every morning. She used a galvanized bucket and we men used milk bottles, each with tea- or beer-colored pee sloshing around the bottom. Mine was normal. The tea color was from Lucky Strike or Chesterfield butts, not from turds from *our* butts, because

Gramma Betsy said, "In that depawtment, we're all on our own." That meant you went in the woods. The toilet paper was hanging from a three-penny nail above the back stoop. You took the roll with you because you never knew how much you'd need. Uncle Thomas said that owls might take a crap on you while you were taking your own, but that never happened to me. My guardian angel must've been watching over me, like a holy umbrella. He also helped me figure out how to go crouching, not sitting. After you used the toilet paper, you stuffed it into the incinerator.

Grampa and Uncle Thomas and their friend Mr. Colarco cut Sheetrock all day and drank beer. After dinner we used lanterns to play poker and listened to the Yankees game on Uncle Thomas's Heathkit transistor. It looked like a miniature briefcase, with holes on one side so the sound could get out.

Red Barber said, "Back, back, back, back . . ." when Tommy Tresh belted a two-run homer. Mel Allen called it a "Ballantine Blast," so we toasted—Grampa and Mr. Colarco with Ballantine, Uncle Thomas with Schlitz, and Gramma and I with strawberry Kool-Aid. When the batteries ran out in the fourth, Gramma shook her head at Uncle Thomas. "Good job making sure to have extras," she said.

The poker chips were red, white, and blue with TMN stamped in gold on each one, for Thomas N. Madden. The M in the middle was bigger because your last name was more important for people to know—just like my school tie said SJA because Joan was the main word of St. Joan of Arc, though it was probably a close call with Saint.

The weirdest thing I found out from using the chips was that Gramma's name had been Madden even before they got married, though of course they weren't brother and sister. (If they were, I mean, talk about huge maculations!) "We're not from Kentucky," she said. Grampa was an Edgewater Madden, and she was a 168th Street Madden.

When I asked what the difference was, she said, "Oh, not all that much. Only looks and intelligence."

"Is dat so?" Grampa said. "Why doncha check in da lobby?"

"This cottage has a lobby?" I said, which made them all laugh.

Grampa explained that his father had his name on a plaque in the lobby of the Empire State Building, the tallest building ever, by far. For the craftsmanship awards, each union got to vote on which member had done the best job, and the pipe coverers chose his dad. He was dead now, but I'd seen the plaque when I was seven. *Peter Madden – Asbestos Worker.* "Yaw great-grampa Pete was the one who taught *me* to play poker, God bless him." He made a fast sign of the cross.

The first few times we played poker the grownups let me use a cheat sheet listing the ranks of the hands. I memorized it in like seven minutes. If anyone disagreed about the ranks or any other rule, Grampa's word was final because he'd studied a book by Edmond Hoyle. That book was the Bible of card games. "Dat's accawdin' to Hurl," Grampa would say. That was that.

In jacks-or-better draw poker, everyone was dealt five cards face down, and you needed a pair of jacks or better to open. But if someone had bet before you, you could raise them with anything. I loved drawing two to a flush or standing pat and raising with nothing. Winning on bluffs was the best because the rules allowed it, so it wasn't a lie or a sin. If another player asked what you had, you pushed your cards into the muck pile and said, "Oh, gee, sorry, I can't remember."

Once Uncle Thomas called my bluff with a pair of sixes. After he raked in the pot he offered me a sip of his Schlitz. "Let the kid drown his sorrows," he said.

Everyone laughed, but Grandma Betsy also said, "What the hell's wrong with you, Thomas?" and pretended she was going to smack him.

I acted like I didn't want a taste. "Schlitz sort of sounds like, you know," I said, and everyone laughed at that too. But I wanted to taste it.

We also played five-card stud: one down, one up, then a third, fourth, and fifth card, all up. Grampa said my worst habit was calling raises with hands like the ace and four of diamonds. I liked to because you needed only three more diamonds out of eleven to make a flush. You could also make A-2-3-4-5, called a wheel. Whenever I won with those hands, he scolded me for being so reckless. "Fold dem hands, Vinny! C'mon!"

"My Gawd!" said Uncle Thomas. "He plays like a Killeen, not a Madden!"

"I *am* a Killeen."

"Yeah, we can see that," he said.

My dad wasn't reckless at all, so Uncle Thomas must've said that because my dad didn't like to play poker. If you asked him why, he'd say, "Buddy, how would it look if the chairman of the fundraiser was gambling?" He wouldn't say it was because his dad couldn't teach him to play, or because his mom and the Jesuits thought playing was a sin. But they did.

"Doncha know the odds against that?" Uncle Thomas asked me.

"Don't be disturbing the kid now," said Mrs. Colarco.

"Why, because he's an Aries?" he asked her.

She was foxy for a mom, but she was always talking about astrology, though she was supposed to be Catholic. When she told Uncle Thomas, "Because he's too busy stacking your chips," everyone howled but me. Poker was supposed to be serious.

Even when you didn't make a flush or a wheel, you could still use a bad hand for bluffing. Plus, if you busted out of chips, you could play Relief Poker. You couldn't bet anymore but could still win half the pot if you had the best hand at the showdown. Then you went back to non-relief status. Grampa said the idea came from President Roosevelt. He said FDR didn't talk about poker during his fireside chats, but sometimes you'd hear him clicking chips together in his hand. His legs were paralyzed, so he couldn't get to the studio as easily as other presidents, so they brought all the microphones up to his second-floor office, which was where he played poker with other Washington big shots. "He clicked 'em together like rosary beads," said Grampa. "Helped da paw guy relax."

Gramma said, "Yaw fulla soup."

"Is dat accawdin' to Sunflower Betsy?" That meant she voted Republican.

"It is." To me she said, "Don't you listen to him, Vince. Don't. You. Listen."

Grampa shook his head like there was nothing to be done about the crazy lady he'd married. To the Colarcos he said, "She tinks FDR was da woist."

Mr. Colarco just nodded. I could tell he was on Grampa's side, but he didn't want to be impolite.

If a kid said something Grampa didn't like, he'd say, "A-rink-a-dink a bottle a ink, da cawk fell out and you stink." When I was little, he used to rub his scratchy chin against my cheek and say, "A-scratchama-cratchama-crora, crama-croy." He said the last part was Irish for "I love you." When he told Gramma he'd do it to *her*, she said, "Mistah, just you troy it!"

When I won half pots from Mr. Colarco, or even whole ones, he'd say, "Well played, young man." His job was building houses. He was helping us build ours "for a little something on the side." He had big gnarled knuckles from handling the wood and the Sheetrock.

He could also do plumbing, but not electricity. Only licensed electricians could wire things, but Grampa was a building inspector in New York, so it was up to him to say who could do what on a project.

Mrs. Colarco said, "He also does anything *I* tell him to."

"Anything?" said Gramma.

"*Any*thing," said Mrs. Colarco.

"Oh, yeah, I'll bet he does," said Uncle Thomas. But I don't think anyone else heard him, because they were laughing too hard about what the women had said. Married people thought some things were funnier than the rest of us did.

The Colarcos' cottage was closer to the lake, and some days I went swimming with their youngest daughter, Margie, who also was going into seventh. She had brown hair, brown eyes, and scabs on one of her knees. One of her elbows had pinkish white spots where other scabs had shrunk and peeled off.

The ruffles fanning out from the bottom of her two-piece blue suit fluttered against my hands or face or other parts (cock) as we practiced saving each other from drowning. She was golden and slippery, which made her even harder to save. Her big brother was a lifeguard and he'd showed her how to hook your arm up and under without choking the victim, and Margie showed me. You didn't want to strangle the person you were saving, of course, but it usually gave me my biggest boners ever. Real doozers. They hurt, plus I think Margie noticed. I had to stay in the water and not look at or think about Margie until they got softer.

When he saw us walking down the rutted, sandy road from the lake, Uncle Thomas said, "Here comes da happy couple!" He let Grampa's car roll alongside us, almost grazing my elbow. "Now Vincent, what've you and Miss Margie been up to? Ta no good, I hope."

"Swimming," I said, keeping my bunched-up towel in front. "Margie, this is my uncle."

Margie stopped for a second, then started walking backwards. Uncle Thomas kept going, which left me standing between them. We were almost at the Colarcos' cottage now anyway, so I just said I'd see her tomorrow.

Back at our cottage, Uncle Thomas was waiting in the driveway, drinking more Schlitz. I thought he would ask me again about Margie, but instead he said, "Whaddaya call a fat dago in a fi-hunnerd-dollar hat?"

"What's a dago?"

"Greaseball *I*-tal-i-an-os. Least most of 'em are. Not your sweet Margie, a course."

"In a hat . . . ?"

"'Spensive, fancy hat." The ash of the Lucky Strike stuck to his lip was as long as the paper part. He put his hands over his head and touched his fingertips together, squinting at me through the smoke. "Great big ol' tall fuckin' hat."

"Abraham Lincoln?"

He shook his head, snorted.

"Yogi Berra?"

"No no no *no*, not no *Yogi*." When he lowered his arms, the ash fell away. Some of it caught on his T-shirt. "No Yankee cuh be one a dese guys. Like dis here dago T."

What? Plus a catcher's mask wasn't a hat . . .

"Pope!" he said, finally.

I got it, but I only pretended to laugh. Pope John XXIII was chubby, but he was also one of the greatest pontiffs in history. His gold and white miter looked expensive, but five hundred bucks? Plus the hat maker would've been honored to make it for free. Only Protestants or a divorced alkie Catholic would tell a joke that sacrilegious. Not that I'd betray my mom's brother, but an altar boy's testimony before a diocesan council in New York *or* Illinois could've been grounds for excommunication. It was so sacrilegious I'd have to confess even smiling.

"Bless me, Father, for I have sinned. My last confession was seven weeks ago."

"Why have you waited so long then, my son?" I could tell right away it was Ted. And I knew that he knew it was me.

"I was on vacation, Father, and that parish didn't offer it on the days—"

"That's fine, my son, I understand. Please go on."

"I have committed the following sins. Talked back

to my grandmother three times, but only to my New York grandmother, Father." I didn't want him to think I'd ever talk back to his secretary. "Had several impure thoughts, skipped English homework one time, told two white lies to—"

"Impure thoughts?"

Jesus! "Yes, Father."

"How many, my son?"

It was probably in the tens or the hundreds of thousands, maybe the millions, but even a thousand was way way too high for an altar boy. "I think about one hundred," I said.

"A hundred, you say?"

"Or so maybe like eighty or ninety?"

"Okay . . ."

"More like ninety."

"I see. Concerning . . . ?"

I was thinking about Margie or Dory or Laura almost all the time now, not to mention movie stars and models, but I didn't want to admit that. You're supposed to confess every sin, even the most trivial venials, but it wasn't really fair that I had to confess them to the same priest I'd served so many Masses for, who was friends with my teachers and parents and grandmother—though I didn't want Fr. Jude to know about them either. Plus getting a doozer from Margie wasn't really a thought. It happened against my will, completely by accident. I just said, "Girls, Father."

"I see. Impure deeds as well?"

G.d. him! "Yes, Father."

"Of what sort, precisely?"

I swallowed. My neck was getting hot, plus my forehead. "Impurely touching. You know, of oneself."

"Where?"

"Down there, Father."

"I see. And how often?"

"Only once. And I'll never do it again, Father. Maybe two or two and a half times, if you count—"

"I see." I heard his chair creak as he leaned back to consider how huge this sin was. Or these sins. "It's so very important that we resist impure urges, my son."

"Yes, Father."

"And the thoughts that accompany them."

"Yes, Father."

"All right. I want you to say two rosaries and make a good act of contrition."

Rosaries? For one or two i.t.o.'s? What would he've given me if I'd confessed to like two hundred thousand? I'd *never* be done saying the g.d. penances! "Yes, Father," I said.

"Go in peace, my son."

"Thank you, Father."

The next time I served for Jude, he asked if I still felt the calling. It was after 8:15 Saturday Mass, when we were still in the sacristy. "Definitely, Father," I said.

"Excellent. You've continued to pray on this then?"

I told him I'd prayed but that God hadn't answered,

exactly. I was nervous because I assumed Ted had told him about my acts of concupiscence. What you said in the confessional was supposed to stay private, but I thought maybe priests were allowed to share information about altar boys who might join their team. Like AAA scouts trading notes about prospects who might make the majors.

Jude put his arm around my shoulder and just like *whoa* started pulling me into his chest—to his armpit. His soutane smelled like cabbage and smoke and BO, and I felt his heart beating. It was normal for him to touch my head, to grant absolution or comfort, but never like this. I ducked out from under him, so I was facing away when I said, "So how can you tell if it's—what's the signal?"

"You might feel the touch of His hand," he said, right behind me. "It often feels like this, Vince." He started massaging my shoulders, then my pits when I twisted away, so it tickled. "If it feels good—just hold on here a second here—that's usually a sign." I was squirming and laughing. The cardboard popped out from his collar. When I said I had to get home for basketball practice, he groaned like, *Since He works in mysterious ways, maybe a ticklish feeling's His way of saying you do have the calling.*

"What's so darn funny all of a sudden?"

"Nothing, Father. It's just—" I pulled away again and ran out of the sacristy.

"Wait a sec now. I said, wait!"

I knew it was a sin, but I kept running for the door.

When he caught up to me outside, we were both breathing hard, neither of us laughing anymore. When he invited me back to the rectory, I said, "Okay, but I still can't go in.

"Still? And why not?" he said, following me across the intersection.

If anyone was watching, they could probably hear us, so I couldn't ignore a priest's question. "My coach'd kill me," I said.

"Your. Coach. Would. Never. Kill. You," he said, liverlips flapping in super slow motion. "So. Vincent. You. Know. That's. A. Lie." But when we got to the rectory, everything speeded back up. "Stay right here," he said, rushing inside.

Whew! I mean, Jesus H. Christ! I almost walked away, but I made myself stand there. Gramma didn't work Saturdays, but since one of her bosses had told me to *stay right here*, what else was I going to do? I thought he was maybe going to get Fr. Ted to come talk to me, but Fr. Jude never came back out and after a couple of minutes I ran almost all the way home.

The next few times I saw Jude he was normal, at least normal for him. Good morning, Vince. Yawn. Good morning, Fr. Jude. *Introibo ad altare Dei. Ad Deum qui laetificat juventutem meam.* We didn't talk at all after Mass because I left from the janitors' door, on the opposite side from the sacristy.

Obviously all priests weren't weird, plus to save my

family from millennia in Purgatory, I'd have to become one anyway. I kept swearing to God I'd never become one of the weirdos. I wished I could look up the statistics somewhere for whether O.S.B. or S.J. had a lower percentage. Either way, to become a priest I'd have to be celibate. To be celibate I'd have to practice self-mastery of the conjugal urges that led to my morbidest i.t.o. days. If that became hard, I'd say extra prayers for the strength to overcome my concupiscence. Because even though concupiscent thoughts weren't mortals, they were dangerous dangerous tinder.

But speaking of conjugal, I'd promised Gramma I would go to St. Stanislaus, though I *could* serve my faith within the sacrament of marriage, as long as I remembered it'd be sinful to use conjugal love as a means of self-pleasure. It was better to think of it as an act of fruitful love of my wife, though I probably wasn't going to have one. But what if I did? The fruit, with the seeds, would be kids. Like St. Joseph and my dad, I'd accept the responsibility of raising them, if that was God's plan. Meanwhile I'd stay pure as a virgin, as St. Joan herself, waiting to give myself wholly to my wife or my Church.

Whichever path I chose, what I'd do from now on was the same: nothing. Keep my hands to, not on, myself. Which would be easier to do if I remembered that Jesus and Grampa Vince were both watching.

At 1:24 p.m. on Monday, October 15, 1962, Sr. Dana taught us in Science, God was creating the perfect conditions to make chlorophyll production go down and carotenoids and anthocyanins go up in the leaves of deciduous trees in our parish's latitude. She actually took us outside for most of the period to show us it happening while explaining how it worked and how lucky we were to live in the Arboretum Village. She made sure we took notes. She was by far the tallest nun at St. Joan, and her voice was by far the deepest.

Because they wore skirts, the girls had to sit on their ankles and feet, on the lawn between the church and the parking lot. They also sat mostly together. I didn't try to move or even crane my neck to be able to see Laura better. What was weird was *all* the girls looked sort of beautiful sitting there in the sunlight, even when Mary Jane Bozak burped, but by accident. When Vogel cut one on purpose maybe four seconds later, Dana hissed, "Hush now, you cretins!"

"You carotenetins," said Vogel, way under his breath.

I closed my eyes and angled my face toward the sun, but kept listening. Leaves had veins just like people did, Dana was saying, to circulate amino acids to wherever they were needed in the body or the tree. Acorns were oak seeds, which squirrels helped scatter so more oaks trees could grow. Maple seeds looked like helicoptery whirligigs called "samaras." When Dana asked why I wasn't writing this down, I told her I was, in my head. I almost said God hadn't created the perfect conditions for me to be actually writing, but future priests didn't talk back.

The sun was still out after school, so the day was already close to perfect when I saw Laura walking down Gamble with Angie. She looked extra pretty as I came up alongside them. When she turned and smiled, she looked even prettier. She brushed her bangs from her forehead, then pushed them back across and kept walking. I'd heard from Phyllis Baumgartner that Laura liked me and from Bianca Eber that she wanted to be called Laurie from now on.

"Hi, Laurie," I said.

She looked at me funny. "Hi, Vince. What's this 'Laurie'?"

"I just heard you want to be called that."

"I did, I do, but who told you?"

"I can't remember. Hi, Angie."

Angie ignored me, probably because I forgot to say hi right away.

"How's Sokol?" I said. I think they both went to Sokol.

"Sokol's fine—Vince," said Laurie. "Or shall I call you Vincent?"

"No. Vinny," said Angie.

Laurie frowned. Making her voice deep, she said, "Hey, *Vinny*!" They both started giggling. "We rilly gotta go," Angie said.

Laurie pushed out her chapped lower lip, like she wanted to keep walking together, but Angie got bossy and they ended up turning left at Center in a way that said, *Walk home your own way*. In second and third and even fourth, we'd all sledded and played tag together, but most fifth-grade girls wanted you to sort of keep your distance or something.

As soon as I got up to my room, I couldn't help thinking about Laurie and Margie. Sometimes we were all three together, and I still called her Laura. Laura in a two-piece in the Colarcos' outdoor shower, Margie in a St. Joan uniform with the knee-socks and pleats at just the right lengths to show off the backs of her knees. Angie's too. We were all getting wet, but none of them cared that I couldn't decide which one to marry. They also didn't mind if I felt a few conjugal urges. Then Angie and Laura got bossy, making Margie unbutton her blouse, show her nipples.

I liked to look at pinup and calendar girls too, at least until I had to officially take the C-vow in June 1973—unless the rector made you take it when you entered St. Stanislaus, in which case I only had till September 1965. The brochure didn't say what those rules were, let alone when they kicked in.

I'd never seen a *Modern Man* or *Playboy* up close, but my new friend Hank Valentine's dad had a Florida Oranges crate filled with mags like *Nudist* and *Swank* and *Sir Knight* in his sawdusty workshop. Hank was already in seventh. He had pretty bad acne and wasn't really too good at sports, but he was still cool to hang around with sometimes. Mrs. Valentine worked at Jewel until 4:45. Even if she popped home early, she wouldn't think to look for us in the workshop, plus only Hank and his dad knew where the key was: in a knothole in the ceiling too far above the water softener for Hank's mom to reach or even see. Hank's dad didn't know that Hank knew.

The workshop was shaped like an L, so Hank and I each had a wing. The sawdust and mouse turds and nails sticking out through the unpainted walls didn't bother us. Sometimes I got half a boner from just the words *Florida Oranges*—from just the idea of what was in the crate, not because oranges were about the same size and shape as nice breasts, whatever damn state they were grown in. Even *Culligan*, the brand of their water softener, could do it.

The good mags were hidden under stacks of old *Readers Digests, Saturday Evening Posts* and all these fishing and power tool catalogs. The best ones had pictures of striptease artists, though *Swank* had better photos of nymphos. If a nympho wore clothes, they were usually torn or her blouse was unbuttoned, sometimes all the way. I looked at them impurely, even at the one of a brunette that reminded me of the time Mrs. Colarco rolled over three treys and two sevens and Uncle Thomas said, "Somebody's got a full blouse." To laugh with a doozer was weird, even if it was just to yourself. Hank couldn't see me, of course. He didn't even say, What's so funny? Because our rule was, No Talking.

Nudist and *Figure Studies* had some good ads for

trusses, but the Special Las Vegas Issue of *Sir Knight* showed stiffer ones offering extra support, which pushed the cleavage up and out even more. I would've been embarrassed if my dad had mags like these, though I was super damn glad Mr. Valentine did. If my own dad had them, not that he would've, I probably wouldn't've shown them to Hank or even told him about them. I wouldn't've told anyone. I wanted to be a good friend by doing unto others, but I also wouldn't want to disgrace a veteran usher behind his back, even though Hank's dad was one too. Whenever he came to our pew with the collection basket and I dropped in my nickel, I knew.

His best ones were *Rapture* or *Slip & Garter*. Even in the shots from behind, these ladies looked good, with the wider straps across their spines and the ribbony straps over their angel wings. The wider straps had the clasps you had until high school to learn how to undo, even though what girl would let you? One *Rapture* I found near the bottom of the crate had an article called "Gimmicks and Gambits to Get Gorgeous Girls," but I didn't have time to read it because Hank's mom was due home in ten minutes and we had to clean up. We stuffed the blue and yellow Kleenex into our pockets and ever-so-neatly restashed everything, making sure the top layer of catalogs was laid out exactly the same as before.

In bed that night I tried to picture those ladies, to make them hold still in my mind. Mostly the ones in *Slip &*

Garter, in their black lacy bras and other dark items of lingerie. That year's Sears catalog only showed white or beige, plus the model never posed sexily or had the right expression on her face. They looked like happy moms getting dressed in the morning. My favorite was the one in *S&G* with brown hair and green eyes in a barn, thinking, "Give me back my saddle and crop!" You knew she was thinking that because that's what the caption said. But my memory of the rest of her wasn't sharp enough, even though it was only five and a half hours later. Plus I couldn't make myself *un*remember that another i.t.o. wouldn't speak well of me so soon after confessing the very same sin the next time I got Fr. Ted or, worse, Fr. Jude.

Before I fell asleep I was tempted to impurely touch and not reconfess, or confess at SS. Peter and Paul, out in Naperville. But in the morning I decided that would be quadruply shameful on top of being a sin of omission, plus I didn't know what I'd say to get someone to drive me to Naperville. Even if I thought of a decent excuse, it'd be another lie I'd have to confess eventually, etc., etc.

Tony Triglio's dad had magazines too. We were shooting baskets with Zrout in Triglio's driveway. He said his dad stashed them in the garage, but he wouldn't say where. "So close yet so far," he told me, as if Zrout had permission to look at them, but I didn't. Asking him again wouldn't help, so I acted like I couldn't care less.

"Holy Rollers like Killeen here," said Zrout, "would squeal straight to Liverlips."

"Or Cardinal Meyer," said Triglio. "My old man'd get excommunicated."

The only reason I was with them was because sometimes the sixth- and seventh-grade teams scrimmaged and our coaches told us to work on our layups and free throws, so anyone with a basket in their driveway had to invite other St. Joan players to share it. But you could tell Triglio didn't want to share his basket *or* his dad's mags with someone in sixth. He and Zrout were saying *fucking* a lot, so I had to too. They were talking about kumquats and boxes and hickeys, and I didn't want to seem like a pity.

When Zrout said Lynn Reidy's mulligans weren't that juicy, I said, "Anything more than a handful's a waste."

"How the fuck'd *you* know?" he said.

I told him I'd felt up Margie's plenty of times, plus her bottom, hips, and thighs. Which I had, in a way.

"Whose?" said Triglio. When I told him, he said, "Don't know no*body* in Lisle named Colarco."

"She lives in New York, where girls are way faster. I was there on vacation last summer."

"Like hell you did," said Zrout. "Her 'bottom'?"

"Oh yeah? Try asking my parents."

"About feeling up my little Margie?" said Zrout. "Okay, I *will* ask 'em."

I knew he was bluffing, so I said, "Go ahead."

"What color were her pubes then?" said Triglio.

"Probably red," said Zrout. "Yeah, they were red. She was on her period and made Needle Dick lick it."

They hooted and howled and wouldn't let up. The more questions they asked, the more it was like, *Use this word in a sentence* on a vocab test. I just made up answers that sounded right. Triglio wanted to know if I knew what fucking even meant. "Of course," I said, though I didn't. At least not a hundred percent.

"How can you be so exact," said Zrout, using two hands to bounce his ball extra hard, "when you don't even know what you're talking about?"

"You can tell by the look on his face," said Triglio. "Sixth-graders usually don't. Like to *talk* big a course . . ."

When Zrout said he knew back in fifth, Triglio said, "That's because my brother told us, and you still fuckin' didn't believe it till you asked your old man."

"Just *tell* him," said Zrout. "Pity-man here thinks you can hear the ocean in seashells."

Triglio stopped dribbling. "You *can* hear the ocean in seashells." It was weird enough having him disagree with Zrout, but super super weird for him to agree with Gramma Grace. "Least in certain big ones you can."

"See?" I told Zrout.

Still looking at Triglio, he told me to "Shut the fuck up."

They argued about it for a couple of minutes, till Zrout called Triglio a *dickfor*. When he said it again, I realized he was talking to me, asking if I knew what it meant.

"What's a dick—" I stopped myself, just not in time.

They cackled and whooped. "Pity wants to know *what's a dick for!*" screamed Triglio, loud enough to hear across the street. He'd served at St. Joan for a while, and Zrout *still* did. I'd served at least seven times with him, though never with Triglio. Not that it've made any difference now, here in his driveway.

"Holy Roller admits he don't know yet?" said Triglio finally. It was obvious he wanted to tell me, to show off how much he supposedly knew about everything.

"If you're talking about the rhythm method," I said, "I know all about it."

That cracked them both up so hard I realized it wasn't the answer. "Wouldja listen to this guy?" said Zrout. "To this sanctimonious little fuckwad?" He started pumping his crotch back and forth. "I'll give you the rhythm method."

Triglio glared down at me. He had stubble on his chin with little pimples underneath, and breath like strep throat. "What's this rhythm method?"

I backed up an inch, or maybe an inch and a quarter. "It's what moms do to not have a baby."

"We're talkin' bout *to* have a baby!" he said, while Zrout, right behind him, said, "D'you even fuckin' know where they come from?"

"From not using rhythm," I said.

"They come," said Triglio, "from fucking. Or in your case, dipstick, from *not*. As I'm sure my little Margie esplained to you."

"Didn't have to, buttwheat. I *knew*."

He shoved me then, using only two fingers. Not hard enough to start a real fight, just to remind me who was in seventh and who was in sixth. When I knocked his fingers off my chest, he put them back on and pressed harder. He knew I couldn't take either of them, which was why it was fingers, not palm or fist yet. When I tried to clear my throat it made my eyes tingle, and I think they felt sorry for me because they were older and it was two against one.

So they told me.

During homework time that night, I was going to ask Ellen if they could be right, but I was too scared she'd mock me, especially if what they'd told me was wrong. She hated all seventh-grade boys, especially Triglio, because he liked to go bow-hunting with his brothers. She once said she'd heard that Ricky had killed a calico kitten with a razor-tip arrow. It went straight through its chest and twanged into a tree, shish-kabobbing the kitten, though its legs kept on moving. I also thought she might not know the answer, even though she was in eighth. I wasn't allowed in her room, but I knew she had a poster saying *Lips That Touch Liquor Shall Never Touch Mine.* Gramma Grace gave it to her, but not the one behind her door that said *Virginity renews itself like the moon,* which she bought at the Book Nook with her babysitting money. Plus even if she did know how babies were made, it wasn't really something you'd ask your sister about. Or your dad, even though Triglio said Zrout had asked his. But I waited till mine got back from his trip to Peoria, and then till after dinner, so he'd be more relaxed. And then till we were almost alone because my mom was upstairs changing Brian. I think Gramma and Ellen were doing the dishes extra quietly so they could listen, so I waited till he left the kitchen and followed him down the back stairs.

"I heard something a couple days ago. About babies?"

He winced. "You did, huh? From?"

When I told him from Triglio and Zrout, he said, "Uh oh," then told me to put on my jacket and went back up to the kitchen. I thought he was going to march me over to the Triglios and start yelling at Tony and his dad, who might get his hunting bow or even a gun, but when he came back down he just took me out to our patio. It was almost November, so taking me outside was the kind of thing he'd only do if he didn't want anyone to hear what we said. He had his martini glass in one hand and was rattling the big silver shaker. I held open the storm door. The iron chairs still had their cushions on them, so we brushed off the leaves and sat down. He took out a cig and snapped open his lighter. "Okay, buddy, let's hear it. What'd they tell you?"

It took me a while to get going, but when he didn't try to rush me it got a bit easier. I was glad it was dark. Gramma kept peeking down from the kitchen, but I knew she couldn't hear us. My dad kept nodding and shaking his head. He groaned when I spelled f-u-c-k, so I started saying *sexual intercourse*. I also could tell he wanted me to keep it short, so I did.

"Well, truth be told, that's more or less accurate," he said. "That's how the spermatozoa find their way up to the ovum."

"The baby seeds, right?"

"Sperm, seeds—same thing. There're millions and billions of them each time, each and every time you—the word is 'ejaculate.'"

So that was why they called it *jack off*. "It squirts up into the—so you and mom *do* that?"

"You bet." He emptied the shaker into his glass. "And then out they come. Only one of them makes it up to the egg." Thank God we weren't close enough to see each other's eyes. "To the ovum," he said.

I realized that if I hadn't promised Gramma to be celibate, intercourse was something I'd do with Laurie or Margie or whoever I'd marry. Mary Mannion, Dory, Jane Pitt . . . but not with Gina Lollobrigida or Marilyn Monroe or the nymphos in *Slip & Garter*—they were just to look at.

"God wants us to procreate," my dad was saying as he lit another cig. "If it feels good, that's just a bonus. Otherwise you shouldn't be doing it."

"I know." Probably not Dory either, I realized. She'd be married before I was ready, though maybe I could invite her to my ordination or something.

My dad blew a smoke ring. He tried to blow another

one through it, but the first one disappeared in the wind. "Least that's what the pope says," he said.

"Yeah, I know."

He asked if I had any other questions. I did, but I said that I didn't. He said "Good" and stood up. I did too. Gramma was gone from the window.

"So there won't be a nuclear war then?" I said.

He didn't look that surprised, which meant I was old enough now to talk politics. "Yeah, it looks like we figured out a way, a way out of—" He dropped his butt onto the bricks and mashed it with the toe of his wingtip. "Though if Khrushchev and Castro keep targeting us . . ."

I was trying to think what to say next, maybe even mention St. Stanislaus, when my mom pushed open the storm door. She shifted Brian from her left to right arm to keep his head inside the house while peeking hers out a little. "Brrrrrr," she said, pretending to shiver.

My dad and I waved and said hi to them. I realized she was probably pregnant again, and thinking about how it happened made me shiver and cringe, no pretending. His boner went into what Brian and the rest of us came out of, though God only knew how we fit. But so then what? What did the screwing part have to do with the rhythm method? When I tried to not picture them doing that, it was the opposite of picturing girls I knew or in magazines. The focus got *too* sharp.

As my dad pulled the door open wider, my mom said, "So what's goin' on out here, fellas?"

She didn't even know that I knew yet.

Detention

For seventh we've got our first not-a-nun teacher, Miss Moore. She's smart so she's hard, though she almost never gives weekend homework. And unlike most nuns, she's strict but not mean. She's not allowed to cane you either. Only Sr. Regina, the principal, can. Miss Moore can still write detentions and rap your knuckles with a three-sided ruler, which John Krawczyk said smarts a hundred and fifty times worse. He said it could rupture a blood vessel or fracture a knuckle, so you'd be in a cast for two months; canings through pants-shirttail-underpants only throb for like forty-five minutes. But Krawczyk—make that Kraw*dick*—is full of it. The pain obviously depends on the caner, the cane, how hard they swing it, how many swings, where they land, corduroys or khakis, etc. Only priests can do it with shirt up and underpants down. Only nuns can cane girls, and never with panties down. "Uh, that'd be my job," John Vogel said when we first heard that rule. "Panties-pull-downer, eighteen hours a day, double shifts." Miss Moore says she won't enjoy hitting anyone's anything, but we won't enjoy it either, so we shouldn't make her do it.

On the first day of school she passed around a sheet of class rules and read them in a soft, soothing voice. Behave as if St. Joan or God the Father is watching, no talking unless called upon, no passing notes, proper uniform attire at all times, three tardies equal one absence, always sit at your assigned desk. Mine's in the first row, far left. Reid Schaefer, our quarterback, sits next to me. Vogel's behind me, and Krawdick sits behind Reid. Vogel, with his shoulders and enormous round head, is our center. I'm a wide end. Krawdick loves football but his parents forbid him to play it because he's only got one kidney.

The girls are on the other side. Only ten boys v. thirteen of them, so they also take up most of the middle.

Miss Moore wears sweaters or blouses and fairly short skirts. You can only get a decent look at her legs when she's up at the board. Her outfits show as much as the girls' uniforms do, though she still writes detentions for too-short skirts or blouses not buttoned up all the way. (Except for the top one. In Religion, Sr. Francona said girls' throats aren't wanton or concupiscent "in and of themselves," unlike breasts, which are a sin of delectation to look at unless it's by accident and only for a couple three seconds.)

Boys mostly get them—detentions—for swearing or horseplay. The closest I've come was when Miss Moore caught me jumping to touch the "207" above our door. "Second time I've told you, Mr. Killeen. Next time I bring out my pad." I almost told her receivers are *supposed* to practice jumping, but my dad would nail me if I got even one, let alone a second for backtalk. My mom would say I'd disgraced our whole family before Jesus and Mary and Joseph.

About once every other week Miss Moore makes Angie Barotka or Misty Bender or someone else kneel with her arms out. Her hem doesn't touch, or she talks back: detention. The pleated plaid skirts are usually long enough, unless the girl's having a growth spurt, but fast girls like to roll them when they think no teacher will notice. You also get the feeling Miss Moore isn't dying to write them for venial infractions, but Regina forces her to—like she'd fire Miss Moore if she didn't write a certain minimum, like a cop's monthly quota of tickets.

Just this morning, she stopped in the middle of a polynomial and stalked back past the globe. "On those knees, Miss Barotka." Angie must've been shooting a beaver—but just to Miss Moore, not a boy. "Oh, maaaan," Angie said, taking her sweet sulky time, while the goody-goods whispered, "What, not *again!*" I swung around, craning my neck. The shoulders of Angie's blazer bunched against her spoiled-brat face. Fat Frankie Boyle sits next to her, so he had the best seat in the house—or would've if he dared to turn sideways. Miss Moore's hip was an inch from his ear, in her stretchy gray wool Friday skirt. She crossed her arms, shifted her weight.

If a buttock or cantaloupe could poke out an eye . . .

"This is how you steward your talents, young lady?" Exactly how Regina would put it.

"I steward?" said Angie.

"How you choose to maintain or present yourself? Keep those arms out and straight."

As the blazer bunched higher, Angie's forehead got redder. I pictured her blurting, "Jeez, look at *your* skirt!" What she said was, "So like, I'm a stewardess?"

As we silently howled, Vogel whispered, "Cane 'er already!"

"Only if you're lucky someday," said Miss Moore. Out came the pink pad. "For now, just a slatternly hussy." Again, what Regina would say. "You'd need to develop some poise."

When Angie mouthed, "Hey, *you're* the hussy," we hooted with respect, disbelief. "Thank you, ma'am," muttered Reid. "May I please have another?"

"Panties down," I said, under my breath. "Right on her talents."

Miss Moore could probably hear us, though not exact words. Otherwise it'd be one of us getting detained, even rulered. "Unroll it this instant," she said.

As Angie adjusted the waist, I stood up to see better. She made sure the plaid hem rode higher, of course. A lot higher.

"Remain kneeling while I write this all up," said Miss Moore. "No one needs to be talking or ogling now. Keep working on problems nine through twelve . . ."

It's her first semester of teaching, not just at St. Joan, and sometimes you can tell she's still nervous. She only got her degree from St. Mary's in June. She's better at History and Math than Religion, which is why for Religion we've got Francona again. Sr. Mary Francupiscence, O.S.B.

English is between Math and lunch. While Miss Moore's diagramming *The young women devoutly pray for peace with the Soviet Union*, she puts *devoutly* on the predicate line, God knows why. She sees me raise my hand out of the corner of her eye, but she doesn't call on or even look at me. She clears her throat and says, "Wait." Not to me, to herself. The mistake's only there for eight seconds before she erases it, draws the diagonal underneath, starts writing *devoutly*. But she made the line too short and her cursive too round, so the last few letters are scrunched like a haywire Slinky.

Vogel whispers, "Devilishly prayed?"

Krawdick says, "Deviantly."

When she turns around, her cheeks and throat are pink, but it just makes her look even prettier. "Sorry 'bout that. Any questions?"

Not even Ruth Ann asks her one. While we copy down the sentence, Miss Moore slide-steps to the left, flexing and relaxing her calves, then starts diagramming the next one.

Reid slides me a corner of looseleaf. *The stewardess gave a piece to the Soviet deviant.* I knew it'd be something like that, so I made sure not to laugh. It seems kind of embarrassing, I guess, but for us, not for her. The next time she turns around I look at her face, in her eyes. Don't stoop, buddy, my dad always says, meaning, Don't stoop to their level—even though when he and my mom got back from parent-teacher conferences last month, he said, "Miss Moore isn't long for our school." When my mom said they'd just agreed she seemed devoted as any nun, he said, "She does, but she's gonna land a husband real soon." "Kev!" my mom said. Ellen, who's a Sacred Heart freshman, gave her usual smirk. "Yeah, we *heard* about her. Hubba-hubba." "I'm not saying," he said. "I'm just saying."

What I'm just saying is, despite my resolution thirty seconds ago to look at my teacher more virtuously, as soon as she swivels to point out a predicate nominative, I can't help noticing the lacy pattern of her bra showing through the side of her blouse, though she probably passes the pencil test. She's explaining how verbs change to agree with plural subjects when she suddenly catches her breath, makes this weird squeak, and backs up.

"Mr. Killeen, please come up here."

What'd *I* do? Did I say "bra" out loud or just think it? Because it's like she was reading my mind, like that kid on *The Twilight Zone* who zapped you for thinking bad thoughts about him. *Stop scrutinizing my lingerie!*

"Chop chop," she says, as I scrape back my chair. "Hustle up."

"Get your ass over there, Duh," whispers Reid. "Hold

out them knuckles."

When I get up to her desk, even though she's wearing her black low high-heels, I'm probably tall enough to be with her if she wasn't my teacher, or even if she is. She can probably read these thoughts too, maybe easier because I'm so close. The thing is, I can't stop them!

The ruler sticks up from her mugful of pens. I wince when she reaches for it, but it's only to pluck out two Kleenex. "Please kill that spider." She points. "Right—*there.*" Laurie shrieks like it's a tarantula or something, but it's just a daddy-longlegs. Not spinning a web or anything, just crouching in the chalk tray, camouflaging itself in the shadow of an eraser. "Use these."

Our fingers touch, and I catch a whiff of soap or shampoo before she backs farther away. When I kill spiders and centipedes for my mom or my sisters, I use two or three, but of course I don't ask for an extra. I zero in, push down, and pinch.

"Got him?"

I nod. People holler and clap, the goody-goods all going, "*Shhhhhhhhh!*" Miss Moore says, "Quiet! Be quiet. But thank you, da Vinci." She smiles.

"You're welcome." I almost say, "Now you don't have to worry anymore, Miss Moore," but that'd be pitiful overkill.

"Uh, Miss Moooore," Krawdick says, "it's *Duh* Vinci. *Duh,*" which cracks people up even harder. If it weren't for the spider situation, he'd've never had the nerve to say it out loud, plus without even raising his hand.

Instead of reprimanding him, though, she asks, "Isn't that what I said?"

"Just wanna make sure you spell it right. Not d-a, d-u-h."

She nods and says, "Ahhh," pretending to write *Duh* on her palm. I shake my head. *Thanks!* I crushed the spider's body, but two of its legs are sticking out, feeling around like they're trying to inject me with poison. As I go to drop it in her garbage pail, she says, "Uh, no. No-no-no-no. Take it to the boys room, please, flush it down, then march straight back in here. No need for a hall pass. Just go."

I don't run but I walk pretty fast, so it takes like exactly a minute. I'm almost back when the bell rings, echoing three times as shrill down the long, empty hall. Every locker is closed, with daylight gleaming off the beige-and-blue tiles, all the scuffs. I've still got two fifths of a boner from touching her finger when the door blasts open and people start rushing out past me.

Not Angie and Misty, however. They squeeze slowly past either side of me, doo-wopping like the Shirelles, "D3 an' Duh Vinci, sittin' in a tree," each letting one cup—Misty's left, Angie's right—brush my biceps. I flex, but too late. "K-I-S-S-I-N-G . . ." Misty smooches the air near my eyebrow, lets me inhale her perfume. They do this about once a month, which I hate but look forward to. I've got less of a chance with either of them than I do with Miss Moore or Miss Universe. A minute from now they'll be sharing short Cokes with their eighth-grade hood boyfriends, who shave and sneak flasks into school. But I do wish I'd worn looser whities.

"First comes love, then comes marriage, then comes Duh Vinci with a ba—"

"Then comes Duh *Vinci*, you mean." I didn't know Reid was behind me.

"You wish," Angie gloats without turning around.

"Ya both do," taunts Misty.

"Duh does, at least," says Reid. "He's also got the hots for D3."

"No shit, Sherlock."

"That hussy!"

"The Singing Nun's just scared of spiders," I call after them, making my voice crack, so I feel even more like a pity.

Miss Moore doesn't sing or play guitar, at least not at school, but her first name's Dominique so some of us call her the Singing Nun. The real Singing Nun's a Dominican sister from Belgium. Her song "Dominique" is Number 1 on the WLS Silver Dollar Survey, even though it's in French. It's not about a girl either. Vogel said that in Belgium and France and their colonies they use the same names for boys as for girls, and vice versa. The song's about St. Dominic, the abbot who founded her order. Her Dominican name is Luc-Gabrielle, but her nickname's *Soeur Sourire,* which is French for Sr. Smile. I've only seen her once on TV, and I guess she smiled more than the average person or nun. She definitely had a big nose. Her wimple covered her hair and the tops of her glasses covered her eyebrows. She didn't look at all like Miss Moore.

The way her eyebrows and lashes swerve outward, Miss Moore looks like Juliet Prowse, Frank Sinatra's fiancée. Both have reddish-brown hair and green eyes, though Miss Moore's more curvaceous. But even when we talk about her figure at practice or lunch, I try to remember that ogling her curves is a sin of concupiscence. She's a devoted teacher and a good Catholic woman. If she was *that* kind of woman, Regina wouldn't've hired her.

At our lunch table, Krawdick says he doesn't see Juliet Prowse but agrees that D3 is curvaceous. "You fuckin' A she is."

"From the Latin for stacked," Vogel says. "*Curvus, curvare, curvaceus.*" He's the one who started calling her D3, for Dominique Double-Deckers. "If laying your teacher's a sin," he says, "then send me to Hell in a hand basket," loud enough for the monitors to hear him. On Fridays it's Feeney, Bonita, Miss Moore.

"Fine li'l teach-ah, waitin' fo' may," Vogel sings, "she just the girl from a-cross the way . . ." Reid sings along while pretending to play the organ. His mom packed him egg-salad sandwiches, and you can see chunks of yolk while he sings. I sing too. But we can't even get through the opening verse because nobody's sure what the words are.

"Louie Louie" is Number 13. The only reason stations can play it is Jack Ely recorded the vocals so

Pope Paul and the FBI couldn't understand them, but he *still* got kicked out of the Kingsmen and the Pope still bans Catholics from listening. The governor of Indiana banned it too, so no Chicago station whose signal reaches over the border can play it. Yet even though Lisle is farther from downtown than Whiting or Gary, some spooky electromagnetic weirdness lets us hear it every time Bob Hale or Dick Biondi announces he'll be spinning it.

Krawdick always says he can top that. His brother Stan drove into Old Town to buy the 45, so John can listen to it on his hi-fi *any time he wants,* as long as Stan ain't around. That's how he was supposed to be able to decipher each word. "This'll settle all arguments," he tells us, handing Reid a sheet of legal paper. For weeks he's been promising to write down the lyrics and show us, and I guess now's the time. "Ladies and quarterbacks first."

Vogel and Rendeck and I swing around to read it over his shoulder.

<u>Louie Louie</u>

Louie Lou-eye, oh no, sayin' me gotta go,
yeah-yeah-yeah-yeah-yeah-yeah,
I said Lou-ay Lou-eye, oh ba-bee, I said we gotta go.

A fine little girl, she's waitin' for me.
She's just a girl from across the way.
She say I take her out, all alone.
She's never the gal I-uh lay at home.

Lou-ay Lou-eye, oh no, I said me gotta go,
aye-yi-yi-yi-yi-yi, baby

CHORUS:
I said, Louie Lou-eye, oh, no
I said we gotta go.

Every night, at ten, I lay her again.
I fuck that girl all kindsa ways.
And on that chair I lay 'er there.
I felt my boner in her hair.

CHORUS

OK, let's give it to 'em, right now!

GUITAR SOLO

Me see . . . Me see: got makeup, remove her clothes.
It won't be long till she slip it off.
I take her in my arms again.
I tell 'er I just gotta lay 'er again.

CHORUS

I said we gotta go now.
I said what's goin' on round here?
Let's go!

But before we can even finish reading, Krawdick starts explaining what everything means. "The singer's married . . . his mistress's name's Mary Lou, nickname's Louie. 'Take her by' means take her by the place where he lays her."

Reid chuckles heartily. "Dickfor, you're *so* fulla

shit . . ."

"Yeah? Ask my *brother.* Jack starts singing 'Me see' too soon, has to wait till the band catches up. But 'fuck her' and 'boner' are why it's been banned."

"And so like, we didn't know this?" says Vogel.

"He's saying he comes in her *hair?*" Rendeck says, way too loud. The pities at the next table—Rogatis, O'Fallon, Vladanka—are obviously listening in.

"In 'er pubes, not the hair on her *head.*" I take the sheet from Reid. "Not in her *hairdo.*"

"Take her *thigh,*" says Vogel, reaching for the sheet, "not her *by.*"

"Take it easy," says Krawdick. "Don't tear it."

"It's in her pubes," I explain, "then it ain't in her *box,* ya dumb douche."

Krawdick looks horrified, even though Vogel's let go and the sheet hasn't torn even slightly. Something stings my left earlobe.

"What's this awfulness I'm hearing?" The voice—her shampoo! "What's *this?*" says Miss Moore, snatching the sheet from my hand.

I try to turn around, but she yanks my ear in the other direction. "What's what?" I say, doing my best not to whimper.

"Is this yours?"

"We found it by the eighth-graders' table."

"Oh my goodness." She's reading it under her breath. "Oh my dear Lord!" She twists my ear harder. "Rest of you weirdos, straight back upstairs!" I've never heard her sound half this pissed off. "Wait by your desks!"

Leaving their desserts on the table, they trudge down the aisle toward the stairs. Sr. Feeney starts herding them. Oh Jeez, how I wish I was with them!

"You, mister, are coming with me. Up, right now. *Up*!"

She lets go of my ear and starts guiding me—shoving me, actually—toward the stairwell. Just about everyone's hissing or clapping or hooting. As Sr. Bonita shooshes the eighth-graders, Angie stands up and yells, "*Way da go, Vinci!*" I pull away from Miss Moore and take the stairs two at a time. She yells at me to stop; I keep going. I only stop at the second landing because I can't think of where else to go. Not that I'd leave the building, but I'm scared I might knock her down the stairs in self-defense. And now here she comes, charging up the last flight.

"You *run*," she gasps, "from a *teacher*?"

"I just thought, we're coming here anyway." I lower my head.

"We most certainly *are*. To the *principal*." She grabs my left arm with both hands and swings me across the hall, pushing me into the glassed-in area outside Regina's office. The secretary, Mrs. Unferth, isn't at her desk, and Regina's door's closed. Miss Moore knocks, tries catching her breath, tells me, "Sit!" Two chairs are piled up with dittos and mail, so I have to take the one by the door. My lungs burn and heave.

It sounds like Regina's in there with a man, though how could Fr. Jude get here so fast from the rectory?

When neither of them answers the door, Miss Moore licks her thumb and pulls back the top carbon, which must be Angie's detention. She checks her little watch and starts jotting: time, date, name, reason(s), number of character points deducted. All hundred?

I can't rat out Krawdick, of course. Once she calms down, she'll see that the lyrics aren't in my handwriting, and maybe recognize his. Not that I'd point out the difference. All it would do is get us both into trouble, not get me out of it. Plus that's how they nail extra culprits. *Tell us your accomplices and we'll go easy on you.* Then they nail you anyway and your friends want to kill you.

When the door opens, Regina looks out, and the man keeps on talking. "Oh, Monique, I'm on the phone, sorry. It's so good you're here. Please come in." The man is just a guy on the radio.

Miss Moore glares down at me. "*Glued* to that chair, mister. Hear me?"

"Yes, ma'am."

In she goes past Regina, who looks past me into the hallway. I don't think she recognizes me, even though I've held the paten under her chin fifty times, seen her tongue sticking out past the gold in her molars. She's taller, more bug-eyed than when taking Communion. She doesn't seem to see me at all.

She closes her door. PRINCIPAL, it says. Not principle. I've always used *Not my pal* to remind me which one means "boss of school." Below the black letters is a faded-green palm frond neatly folded into a crucifix.

My left ear is all pins and needles, so I offer it up for my sins. I could hear better if I cupped my good one against the door, but what if they suddenly open it? Leaning sideways, with less than half a butt cheek still touching the chair, I hear murmurs but not any words. Mixed with the radio, it's all humming buzz.

And then someone says, "Oh my *God!*"

I get down on one knee, not just to hear better but to aim a prayer up at where Jesus's feet would be. I picture the single nail driven through both of them, the blood running down from the wound, which oozes more as He shifts His weight from heel to heel, trying to make it less excruciating. *Dear Lord, who suffered and died for my sins, I beg Your forgiveness for reading banned lyrics, for listening forty-eight or -nine times to a song proscribed by His Holiness, for having concupiscent thoughts about my teacher, impurely touching oneself while picturing her in lingerie I do not know how many times but roughly two hundred, for embarrassing myself and my family, especially my father and grandmother, who as You know heads the fundraising drive and works in the rectory, respectively. I pray for a miracle, that this detention be somehow vouchsafed from me, that I still be allowed to serve on Your altar. Please fill me with Your Holy Spirit and grant me this miracle, one of the first I've ever asked for, Amen.*

I get back on the chair. For the worst detentions, they call your parents and Regina tells Jude or Ted. I'll be out as an altar boy. Definitely suspended, maybe expelled. My dad will completely blow his top, use the belt, make me quit football, ground me till Christmas or longer—like, *Easter.* Jude might give me a hard pants-down caning, on top of the one Regina's about to administer.

The door creaks partway open. Miss Moore slips out, pulls it closed. The pad and lyrics are still in her hand. No Regina, no cane, no detention—not yet. Miss Moore looks jumpy, though not the way she looked with the spider. "Okay, come with me." I get up and follow her, but she swings back around, gets behind me. People rushing back upstairs from lunch turn and gawk. Except for them and for her being behind me, this is how I usually picture us at night: just walking along, looking for a place to make out. I smell her sweat and shampoo as she reaches around me to open our door. "Take your seat." I try to let her go first, but she puts her hand in the small of my back, gentler than I expected. "Go on and sit down."

Everyone's back now and mostly in their seats. Krawdick shakes his head to show how disgusted he is. "I'm dead, right?" I glare: No, jagoff, even though this is mostly your fault. I yank back my chair and sit down.

Miss Moore stands behind her desk, blinking. Knuckles pink and white on the back of her chair. Everyone shuts up and stares. She's the most beautiful woman I've ever seen in real life, and maybe even up on the screen.

"Sr. Regina is about to make an announcement," she says.

What the—?

Reid leans over, reeking of rotten-egg salad. "What the *hell'd* you tell her?"

"Nothing!" I hiss. "Vergina called her Monique and they both disappeared."

The beige speaker above the board crackles. "Boys and girls, this is Sr. Regina. I have some very sad news to report. Our president has been shot. John Fitzgerald Kennedy has been rushed to a hospital in Dallas, Texas." Then just static for a while. A couple of chairs creak, but nobody says anything. "In the meantime we pray for his speedy recovery. Thank you."

Miss Moore asks us to stand, pushing back her own chair, standing up straight, pressing her fingers together. All of our chairs scrape and creak. "Everyone pray with me now. Pray your very hardest for President Kennedy. 'Our Father, who art in Heaven, hallowed by Thy Name . . .'"

One by one, we catch up, though some people talk and don't pray. Even the fast girls are sobbing. Miss Moore's eyes water as I recite along with her, and she looks back at me for maybe two thirds of a second. Reid belches quietly into his fist, to be as respectful as possible.

We're not even done with the prayer when Regina's voice crackles again.

It's way warmer out than this morning—about sixty-five. Sunny, then cloudy, then sunny every couple of minutes.

Probably even warmer in Texas. A beautiful day on which one of the worst things ever has happened. Plus why was he even *in* Texas?

The teachers made the seventh- and eighth-graders walk home with younger siblings, so instead of Laurie or Vogel and Reid, I'm poking along with two pests. Sheila's in fourth, Kevin's in second—both way too young to understand anything. They keep asking what happened, what happened?

"Why'd the man hafta *shoot* him?" asks Sheila, who will not stop crying.

"We don't know yet. Let's try to walk faster, to try and find out."

"But who was it that *did* it?"

"Some guy in Texas. The FBI'll find out by the time—"

"FB*I?*"

"He *shot* him," says Kevin, aiming his trigger finger. "*Ptchew-ptchewww!*"

Before we got dismissed, Rendeck said we'll get hit now by Soviet missiles, though no sirens have sounded. Castro's coordinating with Khrushchev, he said. I keep scanning the sky when the kids aren't looking. They'd never shut up if they knew what might be coming.

Our game with St. Edward's been canceled. Special Masses will be offered tonight and tomorrow. I wasn't scheduled to serve this weekend, and now I can't call the rectory to volunteer. I think Gramma's still there, but I obviously couldn't stop to find out. Regina's there too, I assume, finding out how to handle things. If she tells Ted about my detention, he might not tell Gramma because it would be too embarrassing. Her grandson the altar boy caught with *those* lyrics? That'd go over like a Budweiser fart in the sacristy.

Gramma calls days like this Indian Summer, but it's like God is an Indian *giver*, giving us the first Catholic president and taking him back for no reason. I still don't know if He answered my prayer, but if *this* is the answer, it's the most vicious miracle ever, damning me to the scaldingest cranny of Hell, where traitors to religion and country go. I'll be down there getting perpetually blistered and stabbed in the penis with Benedict Arnold, Judas Iscariot, Geoffroy Thérage, and Thomas and Oliver Cromwell. I'd rather take my punishment up here and get caned by Miss Moore.

Kevin's kicking a pebble, and Sheila keeps dragging her feet through the leaves. Most of them blew off a month ago, but half the front lawns still need raking. It's not till we pass the Armbrusters', whose gutters overflow with oak leaves and twigs, that it dawns on me: theologically, that *can't* be how it works. The miracle, assuming it's been granted, is only that Miss Moore lets the detention slide because of the news on the radio, not the assassination itself. In all the commotion after the second announcement, the crying and questions and even the idiots celebrating as we lined up for early dismissal, Miss Moore never gave me the copy for my parents to sign. She might not've even turned in the top sheet to Regina. *The president's been shot? Oh, my*

God! Oh, and here's this detention . . .

No good Catholic would pray for *any* president to get shot, and God knows I didn't. (Plus what about all the millions of prayers for him to recover from his wounds? A lot of good *they* did. So why would He answer just mine?) But: if a teacher happened to write a detention as an infinitely worse thing was happening a thousand miles away, when she heard about that thing, she might decide of her own volition, with the help of His grace, to grant amnesty or a dispensation or something. It'd just be miraculously good timing, His way of balancing out the hideous timing of her walking up behind five of us just when *I* happened to be holding the lyrics.

Our mom doesn't get up from the couch because she's feeding Brian, watching the news. She gives us big but sad hi's, swallows like she's going to cry. Her due date's December something, but she looks twelve months pregnant. Colleen's on her other side, sipping red Fizzie out of one of her bottles.

"What's the latest?" I ask.

"He said he had a rendezvous with death in Dallas." She gulps. "He took off his glasses."

"His glasses?"

"Walter Cronkite. He got teared-up when he had to announce he was dead."

If Mrs. Unferth had called about the detention, my mom would've mentioned it by now. "They think it was the Soviets?"

"The priests in the operating room said he died of his bullet wounds."

I shook my head, nodded. "The doctor couldn't sew them back closed?"

"Fr. Huber gave extreme unction to remit all his sins. Not that he'd've had many . . ."

"Of his bullet wounds, okay, but who shot them? Whose gun? A Russian's?"

"Oh my gawden of roses—I hope not."

Colleen burps and says, "Ahhhh!" She's giving her Barbie some Fizzie, letting the sticky red juice dribble into their laps. I glance out the window but can't see the sky from this angle.

At the station identification, my mom says, "We'll find out when your father gets home."

Gramma went straight from work to pick up Ellen at Sacred Heart. When they finally get home, Teen Angel heads up to her room—so what else is new?

My mom's making pot roast, waddle-scooting back and forth to the living room to follow the news. She says someone named Lee H. Oswald's been captured by the Dallas police. We'll know more after they do good cop/bad cop, but why didn't they just stop him from shooting the president to begin with?

Walter Cronkite says his body is being flown back to Washington. Vice President Johnson has been sworn into office.

"This monster, this . . . *Oswald*," says Gramma. If

she's heard about the lyrics, I'd be able to tell from her voice. She sniffles and smokes for a minute. "Now this *Texan* takes over?"

Our dad doesn't get home until 6:45, with the bad-week look on his face even as the kids and our mom hug and kiss him. He hardly even laughs when Kevin tries to sack him for being a Giants fan. He says one of his buyers didn't seem too broken up by the shooting, plus he got a flat outside of Danville. After he goes to the bathroom, he comes down to the kitchen to shake up a triple martini, though lately he calls them martunis.

It's against family rules, but Gramma lets him eat on the couch while watching TV. My mom scooches over with Brian.

They're now saying Oswald's a member of the Fair Play for Cuba Committee, though he sure doesn't look like he ever sat on any committee. He's twenty-four, wears T-shirts, and lives in the Soviet Union. C'mon! I want to ask my dad if this proves he was part of a sneak attack by Khrushchev, but he likes to finish eating and pour out Martuni No. 2 before talking serious business.

When a snippet about the Kennedy kids comes on, he puts down his fork. Without looking away from the screen, he lights Gramma's Kent. Except for when he gave me Grampa Vince's mitt and talked about how much he and Gramma missed him and how sad she was that my dad never had a chance to play catch with him, it's the first time I've seen my dad with wet eyes.

But of course that's the signal for everyone else to cry too. Gramma finally says, "Jackie made sure *sniff-sniff* two priests have *gulp* stayed with the body."

"That's good, Mutha," my dad says, lighting a Chesterfield.

"Msgr. Robert Mohan and Fr. Gilbert Hartke. Every second since they took his casket off the plane."

"Jebbies? Benedictines?"

"Fr. Mohan's a Sulpician." She lowers her chin to say, *Look how disappointed I am.* "Hartke's Dominican."

"Hey, just like the Singing Nun," Ellen chirps, while our mom says, "Such a comfort to Jackie."

"The souls of the just are in the hands of a Merciful God," Gramma says.

"I just don't see why," Ellen says, "how He'd let—" She glares at the TV, shakes her head, and sashays upstairs. Let it happen, she was going to say.

To which Gramma would've said, *Ours is not to know the reason why.*

But here's the kicker: Grampa Vince died when my dad was two and Uncle Don was five. John John and Caroline are now in the same situation.

Saturday morning, instead of going to confession as usual, I detour to Reid's house. Whether I'd got Jude or Ted behind the screen, I couldn't've confessed to reading the lyrics without tipping them off about the detention. Not confessing a sin *half* that size would itself be a sin of omission, and maybe a mortal. But if the detention goes through, I can always confess it next week. What scares me right now is that Reid's back from church already, and he might've confessed to reading them with his friends. *And which friends might they be, my son?*

He has on his Notre Dame sweats, though their game today with Iowa's been canceled. He tells me his dad says the Bears are still playing the Steelers in Pittsburgh, but it won't be on TV. We agree that's b.s. They always show NFL road games, but tomorrow's won't be on because of the shooting. His dad says we'll need a distraction by then after missing the college games. "Three lousy hours, he says. How much news can you *watch?*" His dad's a Double Domer, so he knows what he's talking about.

Reid gets his ball and we run patterns for each other in the outfield across the street. His flags and posts have to be shorter than mine because I don't have his arm. My zags and hitches are crisper, but usually he tells me, "Go long." Without any pass rush or DB to hound me, he hits me in stride with a spiral just about every time. I'm walking back, out of breath from a thirty-yard bomb, when he says, "You didn't rat Krawdick out, huh?"

"Aw, man, what, you think I'm a dickfor? *He's* got the dick in his craw for accusing me—"

"What'd your old man say about the detention?"

"He actually hasn't heard yet, with all the commotion. So what about the song? You confess it?"

He nods. "But only to listening. This time, buttonhook at the hash. HUT-hut-hut-HUT!"

A dozen more passes and questions and it turns out he had Jude, who made him say five Our Fathers, make ten ejaculations, and promise not to listen again—almost exactly the same penance Ted gave me last week. Ejaculations are short little prayers, like "Holy Mary, Mother of God, I place my faith in Thee" or "Sacred Heart of Jesus, I place my trust in Thee," but Reid says he switched some of his to "Here comes Ruth Ann Patton, she lays in puberty." She's sort of Krawdick's girlfriend, but Reid digs her too, not that he'd ever admit it.

"I changed some of mine to 'Thou shalt not admit adultery.' He ask you who else saw the sheet?"

"Ah-ah. I almost said, 'Only ten, Liverlips? No problem. Just lend me a few of your *Playboys*.'"

"But only for the articles, Father."

"Thass right." He flips me the ball. "Got your ten ejaculations right here for ya, Jude," says Reid, pumping his fist like he's pounding a three-foot-long doozer.

Jogging home, I realize Miss Moore probably asked me to kill the spider because I was the closest boy—end of the front row, get there the quickest, etc. But I still think I'm her favorite, or was, except for Ruth Ann and maybe Marybeth Marino. Definitely favorite boy. She's given me A's on all three papers so far, A+ on the "Young Goodman Brown" one. She puts little checks next to sentences she approves of, and writes things like *You've made this point wonderfully, Vince.*

Though I've never shown my friends passed-back

tests or papers, when Vogel saw the one with A+ at the top, he said, "Singing Nun's polishing Pope Vince's *ferula*, I guess. Are you speaking *ex cathedra* when you tell her what grade you should get?" In the locker room last week, Reid held open his butt crack and made his voice sound like hers: "Now, Vincent, you *must* desist brown-nosing me." At least he didn't fart in my face. But Krawdick said, "Yeah, ya got shit schmeared all over your schnoz," poking me in the eye as he tried to wipe off the shit with his towel. We both landed a couple of solid shots before Vogel and Reid helped Brother Frank break it up.

So at least they won't be hassling me about sucking up to D3 anymore.

"Lee H. Oswald has been detained by Dallas police until prosecutors can charge him with the felony murder of President Kennedy. He will be transferred tomorrow morning at . . ."

"Godless bastid," hisses Gramma. She must be the one who hung the black sash across the president's picture. Hearing her swear is bizarro enough, but I'm watching TV on the couch while eating a PB&J and nobody says anything? Plus my dad's at the A&P, shopping! What's the world coming to?

The casket, wrapped in a flag, lies in state, right where Abraham Lincoln's was ninety-eight years ago. Long lines of mourners outside, in the rain. Inside the rotunda, priests with rosaries; sailors in spats, with fixed bayonets; oldster presidents Truman and Eisenhower; altar boys with extra long candles. How'd they land *that* assignment? I also can't tell if this is happening right now in Washington or they're splicing in snippets filmed earlier. I dash to the kitchen for milk.

"Bobby would rather be dead than have him be president," my mom says.

"Disciple of Christ, whatever he is," Gramma says. She's too mad to cry anymore. Eyes glaring, smoke blasting from her nostrils, she looks like a dragon with a freckly bosom.

"It must be God's will," says my mom, "though I still don't see how . . ."

"All I can say is, no other leader would be blessed with *half* this much clergy."

On my way upstairs, my mom says, "Oh, Mrs. Unferth called," and I stop. Before I can even get nervous, she tells me school's been canceled till Tuesday because the funeral got moved up to Monday. Ellen's door opens immediately. "Sacred Heart too?" she shouts down.

"Haven't heard yet!" my mom yells. "Banks will be closed, so I'd think so!"

Back up in my room, I keep 'LS on 3 while going over the reasons to think it won't go or hasn't gone through yet. If Regina got her hands on the lyrics, I'm done for; Miss Moore still has them and I might have a chance. She knows I didn't write them, which has to help calm her furies. Five guys passing it around, Vince loses at musical chairs—at musical pass-the-banned-lyrics.

If possession's nine tenths of the law, what's . . . detention?

Vengeance is mine, saith the Lord, not Dominique's. She's also more likely to forgive and forget over a three-day weekend than if we went back on Monday, I think.

New teachers don't know every rule yet. Mrs. Unferth's in charge of procedure but wasn't in the office when we were. Regina was way too distracted. No one's called my parents about it.

Being an altar boy could help me or hurt me. We're supposed to set an example, meet a higher standard, etc., so me getting caught with them could be considered worse by Regina or Jude than if one of the hoods did. They might want to *make* an example . . .

That Gramma works at the rectory and her son leads the fundraising drive might stand me in good stead, as he'd say. But if they cut his son or her grandson any slack, it'd be unfair to all other students.

I think I can handle getting caned by Regina, even by Jude with my pants down. When Phil Dixon got caned by him for punching out Mike Waligora two days before they graduated, it just made Phil seem even cooler. Everyone said he didn't cower or complain but just took it; he *smiled*. (Though how could they know this if it happened in Jude's private office?) But if I get expelled, or suspended from serving, for being stupid enough to get caught with banned lyrics, no one would think it was cool—the lyrics maybe, but definitely not getting caught.

Miss Moore gets the caning assignment and it makes it a whole different ballgame. I'm afraid that I might get a doozer.

When it comes on at 10:45, I'm in bed, even though it isn't a school night. I dial down my Zenith to 1½ and hold it against my good ear. I can't remember exactly what Krawdick wrote down, but his only mistake seems to be in the chorus, where Jack doesn't sing "I said" every time. Pretty close, though.

I turn off the Zenith and try to fall asleep, but I've still got it stuck in my head. I've also got to disagree with myself that Monique is too old to ask out. It won't be that long, three years and four months, till I can take her by Tops Burgers in, say, a T-Bird convertible. Save up for it by caddying, playing poker, maybe inheriting the rest from Uncle Barry, who suddenly dies of no-pain cancer out in Montauk. Or buy it now and let *her* drive to Tops.

She lets us hold hands, maybe kisses me goodnight when I walk her to her door. Lips closed at first, then slightly open. Or we stay in the T-Bird but move to the little backseat after putting the top up. Sometimes she likes to rassle like Elly May Clampett, grow her hair longer like that, wear tight dungarees. If I try anything, though, she scolds me for my "dirty mind" and "forward comportment."

Though it's back in the forties, my dad and I wear our blue Dacron suits to nine o'clock Mass. His idea, but why argue? I'll need him on my side any day now. With our maroon ties (for St. Joan and his old Fordham Rams) we're practically red, white, and blue. We're taking his Olds, to get there in time to save a pew for the ladies and kids, who were taking too long to get ready.

He's far from over it, but at least he doesn't have bloodshot eyes anymore. He talks about how he and Uncle Don, the Kennedy brothers, and I have all served on God's altar. "You're up for next week, right?" The schedule's not out, but I nod. "Keep it going, buddy," he says. "Kevvie's next." When I tell him I've already taught him the *Introibo*, he tugs my lapel.

He parks and heads off with the ushers while I rush to get dibs on a pew. Most of the early birds look pretty solemn, anxious to hear what our pastor has to say because everything's been so confusing.

Five minutes later the rest of our family crowds in, the ladies dolled up like it's Easter: my mom in her navy wool pregnant coat; Ellen in mascara and lipstick, like she's going on a date in the city; Gramma in her beaded black dress and net veil, and of course her fox stole.

By the time Ted emerges from the sacristy, people are lining the walls. Flynn and Donohoe, eighth's biggest Holy Rollers, are serving. *Introibo ad altare Dei,* etc. The Barotkas have squeezed in across the aisle, three pews ahead of us, Angie at the end in a blue skirt four inches above the backs of her knees. So it won't seem like I'm ogling, I pretend to adore Station X, a carving of Jesus being stripped of His garments, on the pillar above her dad's head.

Ted barrels along, saying some lines before the servers can finish their response to the last one. *Agnus Dei, Filius Patris* . . . If I squint I can see Station XII. Not that I can make out the carving from here, but I know it shows His death on the cross. As Francona likes to say, *Don't despair, one thief was saved; don't be presumptuous, the other was damned.* I see Angie kneeling before the congregation, her back to the altar, arms held straight out; crucified in only a loincloth, with no crown of thorns and ropes instead of nails, like the thieves, being scolded and scourged by Miss Moore: *this* for your backtalk, *this* for that skirt, *this* for your wayward comportment. My doozer's so hard that it hurts.

When Ted finally gets to the rostrum he already looks tired, more salt than pepper, though after the sermon he still has to give Communion to like two hundred people. Gramma loves him so dearly, she sighs.

"We are stricken this morning by the assassination of our beloved fellow Catholic, John Fitzgerald Kennedy. Many millions the world over join us in lamenting his untimely death." He mentions twelve Catholic countries, even some Protestant ones. "Some will ask, 'Why does God countenance such tragedy?'" He pauses to watch all the head-shaking. "Then we remember His only begotten son suffered a miserable death to cleanse mankind of its sins. This teaches two important lessons.

First, that suffering is never wasted. And second, to always trust that God the Father knows best." Gramma fingers her Sacred Heart scapular, nodding and shaking and weeping.

"John's devotion to country and Church were equivalent, one and the same. He served both by valiantly fighting for freedom of religion in the Pacific, in Cuba, behind the Iron Curtain. But now a godless coward, a Communist cur, has cut down our John, and we seek the Lord's justice. There's an appointed time for everything: a time to weep and a time to mourn; a time to be born, a time to die; a time of war, a time of peace; a time to love, a time to hate; a time to heal, a time to execute.

"We also pay tribute to John as a husband and father, a good Catholic family man. The demands of the presidency often took him abroad, as when he visited his Holiness this past July. Yet he always made sure to share with his little son and sweet daughter whatever time was his own, mindful as well of three other souls in the Nursery of the Kingdom of Heaven, each delivered from Limbo through the sacrament of baptism. They are fatherless now, though not spiritually." The parents in front of us, especially dads, nod and murmur. Moms weep. My mom and Gramma act like they're in a heaving and sniffling contest.

". . . always at his side, gracious Jacqueline. Always true to the obligations of wife- and motherhood, she gave new dimension to the role of First Lady. Her pink outfit now stained forever with the blood of her husband, Divine Providence blessed her by allowing her hero the comfort of dying in her arms." Which reminds me of when Marilyn Monroe sang "Happy Birthday" to the president just before she died, and Gramma said, "Jackie'll be positively green-eyed."

Donohoe's yawning, trying to hide it by making his eyes extra pious. Flynn thumbs the zits on his neck. Fr. Ted's sermon must be a homily, I guess, because diocesan law forbids eulogies during funeral Masses. Plus I still can't decide whether to take Communion with unconfessed sins, a couple of which might be mortals. If I don't, though, I'll have to explain why I didn't.

"This morning, even though his body is yet to be interred, John speaks to us in the words of St. Paul: 'As for me, my blood has already flown in sacrifice. I have fought the good fight. The reward of heaven will be granted unto me, as to all those who welcome His coming.'" Fr. Ted pauses, gazing at the nave, just like always. Gramma knows what's coming too, and she whispers along with her boss: "Eternal peace grant unto John, O Lord, and let perpetual light shine upon him, in the name of the Father and of the Son and of the Holy Ghost, Amen."

While my dad turns in the collection money, I wait at the bottom of the steps, two yards over from the famous blood stain. You can still make it out—grayish maroon, shaped like Italy—after dozens of scrubbings, from the most humid Sunday of July, when Ruth Ann's grandmother fainted while standing at the top of the steps, knocking her dentures and most of her teeth out. Five days later, she died of a hemorrhage. Our family had always waited right there, ever since my dad became an usher. Now we wait here, a couple three yards to the right.

My mom had to pee, so our other car's already gone. So's Angie and everyone else from my grade. The day's just too dismal, I guess, for after-Mass chitchat. Cars keep arriving at the curb to pick up the oldsters. Everyone left is talking about the Bears or Lee Oswald. "Sauté his Red balls," one dad says. "Chair's way too good for this twerp."

The sun's like a flashlight behind the low blanket of clouds, though it could also be God watching over me, still trying to decide whether to grant me my miracle. If an ICBM is headed this way, you couldn't see it because of the clouds, plus the shear of light comes too fast to shield your eyes anyway. With mortals on my soul, unless we shoot it down before the warhead detonates, my skin'll melt here and/or in Hell when I die. The same difference, I guess, except that the melting in Hell lasts a trillion times longer. But my ear hardly hurts anymore.

I finally spot my dad coming down the steps—with *oh Jesus* Miss Moore! She must've been way in the back and, like me, skipped Communion. She lives out in Naperville, so her parish is Peter & Paul, but so why's she at *this* Mass? She and my dad are shaking their heads, solemn as all get out, though they seem to relax as they reach the last step.

"I believe you know this young scoundrel," he says. He's dying to ask, *No Communion?,* but he'll wait till we get to the car.

"I do," she says, friendly but sad. Her left shoe is right on the stain.

"He tells us so many good things about you."

"I'll just bet he does," she says, pulling up the collar of her trench coat. Her eyebrows go up too. "Like father like son, eh?" she says, complimenting or mocking our suits. "Did he say he killed a spider for me?"

"He *did*, huh?" Like killing a spider has a double meaning, or like he's flirting with her—or *I'd* been, by killing it for her. "When was this?"

"On Friday." Her sad voice again. "Just before, you know, we heard."

Well, not *just* before, I think. She squints like she's reading my mind again.

"Must've been something," he says. "Having to announce or explain that."

"I couldn't *begin* to explain it—except to say what a terrific role model he was for our boys." But she never said anything like that! When she looks back at me, holding my eye, I hear a low rumble. I also hear "Drip Drop" by Dion.

A man in a black Corvette is looking over at us from the curb. Thick brown pompadour, green pilot sunglasses, younger than my dad. Almost like a greaser version of the president, with sideburns, had arisen, after only two days, from the dead. He's got the top down, so the heater must be cranked up on high.

My dad turns and looks as another dad whistles. "Triple-black," says a high school guy behind us. "Sisty-one ducktail."

"Okay, here's my ride," says Miss Moore. "Kevin, you have a good day, if that even makes sense anymore."

"It does," says my dad, cupping her elbow. "You too."

"And say hello to Mrs. Killeen. Vincent, I'll see you on Tuesday." All pretty friendly, unless they both deserve Oscars. All three of us might, come to think of it.

She walks toward the Vette in slow motion: mysterious bombshell in trench coat, in one of those dirty French movies. As she reaches for the handle, the man leans across to push the door open. They both have brown hair, so it could be her brother; I'll have to find out if she has one. She dips and slides in, and I make myself look up away from her stocking, the kind with the seam down the back. She's never worn that kind to school.

"You," says my dad, "are one lucky guy."

She settles into the seat, which I'm glad is a bucket. Dion keeps singing, "Heh," so that's what I say to my dad. What else am I going to tell him?

"Drip Drop" ends as the Vette rumbles off from the curb. She waves; we wave back. I won't be surprised if the next song's the one that caused all the trouble, though it might get me out of it now. I hear the organ's

3-2-3 rhythm, the drums, the first words. They keep it on 'LS all the way to wherever they're going and it's bound to come on any minute.

Holy Week

Palm Sunday, March 22, is also my birthday. I don't think Fr. Ted knew that, but he still gave me and Gramma braided strands of palm he had personally blessed. We were on the sidewalk between the school and the sacristy, right after I served his eleven o'clock. When he apologized for not having an extra one for Ellen and asked me to share mine with her, I said, "Of course, Father."

"That's okay, Father," said Ellen. "Forget it."

Forget it, right to Fr. Ted's face! Sort of like saying, *Get bent, Fr. Ted*. He raised his eyebrows and adjusted his horn-rims. Gramma looked at the sidewalk, too embarrassed to even try to make an excuse. Some things are just inexcusable.

The palms were so new they were shiny green-yellow. Rameaux tresses, Gramma called them while driving us home, spelling out the first word. Ellen had called dibs on shotgun, so I was in the back seat by myself—on my birthday!

"In Ireland," said Gramma, "they used to use goat willow. In Scotland it was evergreen sprigs."

Ellen looked out her window and exhaled, shaking her head so minutely you'd miss it if you weren't on the lookout. In Lisle we used to care, she was saying. In Lisle no one gives a shit, really.

As soon as we got home, she stalked up to her room. Gramma took the St. Patrick's Day banner down from her mantel and used the same tacks to hang the palms next to each other. She asked my mom to snap a picture, making sure both new palms showed between us. When my mom said, "Say cheese," I said, "Jeez," because Gramma was being annoying. Both of them were—big surprise. "One more, just one more" they kept saying. When I finally got up to my room to start homework, I kept seeing spots from the flash cube.

And now, like for all Sunday dinners, Gramma leads us in grace, though at least no one's taking more pictures. She stubs out her Kent, twines her bony fingers together, stares at her plate until people stop blabbing. "Bless us, O Lord, and these Thy gifts, which we are about to receive through Thy bounty, through Christ our Lord . . ."

We all say "Amen," except for you know who. She barely lets her fingertips touch while murmuring a couple three words but only so if my dad yelled at her for not saying grace she could snip, I just *did.* Since she turned fifteen back in January, she's been too busy acting like she's John Lennon's girlfriend to pay attention to things like palms, Lent, or grace. She cut her bangs straight across her eyebrows and started wearing makeup and the shortest skirts she thinks she can get away with, though everyone keeps reminding her that the John Beatle's married, not to mention eight years older than her. Some days she and our mom shriek at each other for hours on end; if our dad's home that night, they keep it up after dinner, two against one. He even grounded her two straight weekends for a paisley skirt she'd rolled up at the Valentine's hop he chaperoned, but it *still* didn't stop her. She already has the straight, blondish hair, just not long enough yet for the mod look she's going for. As if she'll meet *any* of the Beatles, or they'd ask her on a date if she did. *Meet the Beatles!*, the LP she's just about worn through the grooves of, is as far as she's going to get. But these days no one can reason with her. When she and her friends Dory and Gina see them on TV, they quiver and scream and start crying, hardly even listening to the end of the song. Everyone else can go scratch. The only thing not completely spastic about them is that Dory and Gina happen to be the most bodacious Sacred Heart freshmen by far, so it's cool they hang out at our house. "Let's head to Duh's after practice," Vogel says every day at 3:20. "See who there might be to see." Problem is, you only get to see them in the kitchen or the hall outside Smellen's lair. Almost all Sacred Hearters act like seventh-grade boys don't exist, but not Dory. When she sees me on the stairs she musses up my hair and says, "Still diggin' this dry look, kiddo." She'll barely touch my ear for a third of a second, but her aura's like dryer static, snapping and clinging to my clothes and my face, but not in a way that's annoying. More like the opposite of. If I try to say anything it zaps into my mouth and collects at the back of my throat in a crackling lump. I can't swallow. It usually lasts till I get to my room, lock the door. Unless my friends are with me, she never fails to give me a thermonuclear doozer. Detonation of warhead imperative.

All Gina does is mock us, blowing us kisses or asking, "So how's Domineeeeque?" Either that or ignore us. So how's about blowing me is what I should tell her sometime. I'm sure it'd go over real big.

Anyway, because it's my birthday, I have to drink the blood after grace. It's supposed to honor the birthday person and give thanks for our family having enough to eat. We eat of His body and drink of His blood every Sunday, my dad is reminding us, but during Lent it's more sacred. He carves a few slices down to the rarest part of the roast, lays down his new cordless knife, takes a drag of Old Gold. "All righty then . . ." He positions the Waterford goblet and picks up the platter. Making sure the meat doesn't slide off the end, he tilts the platter just far enough to let an inch and a half of bloody juice trickle down into the goblet. The one we've been using lately is like a glass chalice, with crisscrossing diamonds etched in. The Donegal hock, Gramma calls it. But hock as in big fancy goblet, not as in hock up a loogie for suckers to drink by mistake.

"Today Vince becomes our second teenager," says my dad. "Please pass this over to him."

Gramma beams as she passes it, using two hands, touching only the base and the stem, as if the rest is too holy for a woman to touch, or any nonpriest for that matter.

"Oh dear," says my mom, "we've got two of them now?" Like she's surprised to hear I'm a teenager after squeezing out "13" in blue frosting.

"Afraid so," says my dad.

Also using both hands, I hold the hock up to the light. The blood makes the bowl seem encrusted with rubies. *"Hic est enim calyx sanguinis mei."*

"Novi et aeterni testamenti," says Gramma, joining in on the joke, in a way.

"Haec quotiescumque feceritis," says Kevin. "In something *memoriam* something."

"Mysterium fidei," I say, in a deeper voice, like Fr. Ted's.

"Not to mention being chosen to serve High Mass on Eastah," says Gramma. I thought she was going to add *And deciding to enter the seminary.*

Almost everyone claps. "Hear hear!" "Happy birthday!" "Amen!"

"Oh my Gawd," Ellen says, "such an awnuh!"

"Fir-teen?" Brian says.

Kevin holds up ten fingers, then three, helping

Brian count them out.

The blood is lukewarm and clotty by now, so I swig as much as I can past my taste buds. Instead of saying F-you to Ellen, which would cost me my presents and at least thirteen smacks from my dad, I knock back the rest in one gulp and go, "Ahhhhh."

After dinner the littler kids clear the table and Gramma lights thirteen candles, using the last match to start a new Kent. Kevin's already singing as he carries the cake from the kitchen: ". . . 'cause ya look like a monkey, and ya smell like one too." While everyone else sings the right words, he yells, "Don't forget to make a wish!"

After considering a hi-fi, I wish for a second-base feel off of Laurie, then blow them all out with one breath. I doubt I'll get even to first before the summer after eighth, when some of the less fast St. Joan girls start to put out, if they ever do. I've prayed plenty of times for Laurie to let me kiss her, but a feel isn't something you'd pray for. Not just because it would be sacrilegious—because it might majorly backfire.

"So what'd ya wish for?" says Kevin.

I wink and say, "I forget," which gives me a better idea: maybe Margie will kiss me this summer. My voice might stop cracking by then, and she'll see how much taller I am.

My mom cuts the cake—white with chocolate frosting—then slides the lopsided cubes onto *pink* paper plates. Sheila's passing out the plates and plastic forks while Gramma and Kevin pile the presents in front of me. He holds up what's obviously a football wrapped in green paper. "I predict he likes this one the best." From the sizes and shapes of the others, it's clear I ain't getting a hi-fi.

From my mom, a crew-neck blue sweater, adult M. From my dad, shaving cream and a razor I wish I needed more than I do, though shaving every day with fresh blades is supposed to make the hairs come in thicker. From "The Kids," though no doubt bought by our mom, *The Night They Burned Down the Mountain,* which I've already read, and *The Edge of Tomorrow.* Thank you, you're welcome, etc., but Dr. Tom Dooley, you're boring! The football's from Great Uncle Jack, an official—and slippery—Wilson NCAA model with white stripes on either side of the laces. No card, though. No money.

"Short look-in on three," I tell Kevin, finding the laces, "hut-hut-*hut*." I hit him in the belly for a couple of yards as he dashes into the living room.

"Ditka drags him across the goal line," he yells, stiff-arming a tackler and diving into the couch, *"for a touchdown!"*

My mom and Gramma moan, shake their heads while my dad and I clap. Ellen claps too and says, "Yay!"

Bouncing back up, Kevin yells, *"As the Bears become the '63 champs!"*

"Rah rah, go team," Ellen says, with a fake cheerful smile. So f. her.

From Gramma Betsy, Grampa Tom, and Uncle

Thomas, it looks like I'm getting more books. Taped to the wrapping is a card with a black cat electrified with fear of a "13" made of five lightning bolts. Inside it says, "Good Luck on Your Birthday" above their three signatures—and a one, a two, and a ten-dollar bill. Oh my *God*.

"Free dollars?" says Colleen.

"Thirteen," I say, unable to believe it myself. "I guess, I just—wow."

"Wow is right," says my dad.

Gramma sniffs and fake smiles. Ellen's doing her best not to look jealous, even though it would take her less than a month of babysitting to make thirteen bucks. I'm still too young to caddy *or* babysit.

When I unwrap the present, it turns out to be a pair of Bicycle decks laid side by side on top of *The Education of a Poker Player*.

"Oh, my dear Lord," Gramma says, then something else under her breath. She shakes her head, blessing herself.

My parents are silent so far, but it's clear they are taken aback. Way aback.

The author's picture is on the front cover, right at the top, next to HOW TO WIN AT POKER! Wearing cufflinks and a tie, he looks like a cross between Alfred Hitchcock and ex-President Eisenhower. Below the title it says, "A lusty, funny, cool, and knowing introduction to the great American sport by one of the great masters of all time - Herbert O. Yardley." He's smoking and playing five-stud, using his right thumb to lift up the corner of his hole card, *and he only has three other fingers!* His smoking hand has four, plus a thumb.

"Cooooool!" Kevin says, then gives me a scared secret glance. We both know he shouldn't've said that.

The book only cost fifty cents, but except for the thirteen bucks it's my favorite present by 24,900 miles, though of course I can't say that out loud.

"Jesus, Mary, and Joseph," my mom finally says. She reaches past Ellen and holds out her hand till I have no choice but to give her the book. She glares at the cover and hands it to my dad, still shaking her head, like Herbert O. Yardley's the devil incarnate and her parents are almost as evil.

"Great American 'sport'?" says my dad.

"Grampa Tom says if chess is a sport, so is poker." It was actually Uncle Thomas who said that, but none of the adults here are the president of his fan club; in fact, his own sister might not be even a member. "It's what President Roosevelt played instead of golf."

"FDR was paralyzed, buddy. Otherwise . . ."

"He was always a swimmer," my mom says.

"But isn't that how he *got* paralyzed? Plus Grampa says he clicked his poker chips together while giving his fireside chats."

"He did no such thing!" huffs my mom. So her dad is a liar, she's saying? Everyone gets kind of quiet.

"Poker's not a sport," says my dad. "Here to tell ya . . ."

When Ellen says, "FDR was a swinger?" it looks like we've got one of their three-way six-hour fights to look forward to, till Kevin shouts, "Golf's not a *sport!"*

"Kevvie!" says my dad, holding open his palms. "Sammie Snead? *Arnie?*" Our mom, whose face is all red, keeps glaring at Ellen, who finally shrugs, looks away. Dead silence.

Happy birthday to me. Happy birthday to me. Happy birthday, da Vinci, happy birthday to me.

My mom keeps on glaring at Ellen, but my dad has gone back to thumbing through my book, pretending he's just disappointed, not mad. He's never come right out and told me, *Don't ever play poker,* but he always says he and his dad never did, at least not for money. "As long as you don't ever play for anything but matchsticks or pennies." Like pennies aren't supposed to be money? And ever since the Maddens taught me to play, their daughter's been even more against me playing than my dad is. She and Gramma Grace call decks of cards "the Devil's Playground," which is why when I play at Vogel's or Krawdick's house I never mention it at home, even though I'm up seven bucks.

"And buddy," my dad says, "I don't think they knew you gave it up for Lent. So maybe you can have this next Sunday."

I fucking can't believe it. "I—maybe *next Sunday?"*

"Isn't that what I said?"

"But it's mine . . ." Making sure not to whine, I exhale, start again. "It's my present from Gramma and Grampa."

"For which you can wait one more week."

"But my birthday's *today.*"

"And you can wait one more week for one gift. This of all weeks, you can wait. Meanwhile, that sawbuck goes straight in the bank."

"But so why can't I—*sheeeez!*"

"Oh, my gawden of roses," says Gramma.

"No one *else* has to wait for their presents!"

With his not-kidding look, he says, "Watch the tone, birthday boy."

The other kids have gotten all quiet, until Smellen repeats "no one *else* has to wait" in her girliest pity voice. Almost everyone laughs, even our dad for a second. "Poor boy's gotta wait for his *pwezent?*"

"That tone too, missy," he says.

She doesn't look down or apologize. She stares straight ahead, waiting (I know) for him to look away before she starts rolling her eyes. Meanwhile Gramma has pushed one last present, from her, toward my plate. Wrapped in green foil paper, it's longer but thinner than the Yardley book. I open the envelope, pull out the card: a baseball player swinging a bat. Inside, he connects with the pitch. HOME RUN ON YOUR BIRTHDAY! *Love, Gramma.* No money, no check. As I peel off the paper, she says, "This is the most precious thing in the *world* to me, deah, the *most* precious thing."

"I thought it was the ring you're saving for Ellen's wedding," I say.

"Well, that too, of cawse. This is something I want *you* to treasure."

"Okay . . ." It's another damn book. Even worse, this one is used. No writing or picture on the front or the back. Drab olive cloth, rounded corners.

"It's your namesake's service diary from the First World War."

"Thanks, Gramma." What else can I say?

Ellen's pretending she couldn't care less as I open the book that's supposed to be so g.d. precious.

Vincent L. Killeen

21 Leah St.

Providence, R.I.

Foreign Service Aboard The U.S.S. Baltimore
1918

3/4/18 On this day at 2:30 p.m. we got underway from New York Harbor for the much looked for trip to "Some European port." 'Twas a relief, for the past two months were spent in oftentimes tedious preparation. The ship has been overhauled from top to bottom. Stores sufficient for six months were taken aboard.

About two hours before starting our attention was called to the British cruiser Leviathan, for she passed our port side scarcely a hundred yards distant. Majestically she passed and a farewell wave and cheer went up from about 13,000 soldiers. She could hardly be recognized by the camouflaging.

It's written in black ink on buff paper, the blue lines ruled closer together than modern-day looseleaf. His tidy penmanship is sort of like Gramma's, but different enough to prove she didn't write it herself, though they both say things like "scarcely" and "'Twas."

3/5/18 We are proceeding eastward at the rate of 12 knots per hour. It is payday, but no money is in evidence. A slight pitching of the ship is noticeable.

3/6/18 All hands are paid. The day is clear and water calm.

3/7/18 Arrived at Halifax, Nova Scotia. Upon entering the harbor a great quantity of ice is on the water. Preparations are made to coal the ship.

3/8/18 A snowstorm is at the zenith of its glory, and the thermometer registers 8 degrees below zero. Took on 147 tons of coal. At 3 p.m. there is a shrill blast announcing that we were on the last lap of our journey. Hardly had the echo died amongst the hills before it was noticed that we were to be accompanied by the Leviathan. The band aboard the Leviathan played "The Star-Spangled Banner" and the popular air "Over There" as she drew near us.

It's easier to follow the more I get used to the handwriting. I feel the kids and adults all watching me read. Even Ellen doesn't pretend not to be when I finally look up.

Gramma hovers above me. "I can't wait to hear what you think of the Holy Week entries."

"Any big battles?"

"Of cawse. The Northern Lights, Jebbies, aeroplanes, tanks . . ."

"Tanks in the *navy*?"

"Tank practice in Glasgow," my dad says. "Submarines, minelayers, baseball games with that same glove we saved for you . . ."

"Five-paragraph book report due Monday morning," says Ellen.

I put the new decks—one's blue and one's red—in my smallest desk drawer, on top of my old decks, along with my tally sheet and bankroll. With the deuce and the single, it comes to $11.49—$21.49 till I have to put the ten in the bank. Which I can't do till Saturday because I'm in school during bank hours, or at basketball practice. Plus on Saturday we're away at St. Mark's.

My dad is obviously an asshole for keeping the book. Giving up poker for Lent was conveniently his idea in the first place, and now he acts like reading about it's the same thing as playing? At least he could've let me read the part that explains what happened to Yardley's middle finger. I also have to remind him that the dads of the parish played poker at the holiday fundraiser *he and Fr. Jude were in charge of.* That's what gave Vogel the idea to start having games at his house, where *his* dad lets us use his cool old eight-sided table, with the slots for your chips and sodas—or beers. If poker's supposed to be this big sin, why do they send fliers around to get dads to play it in the St. Joan church basement, a few feet below the altar? Plus they play it all over the diocese!

But the thing is, if I bring that stuff up, it won't change his mind. It'll just remind him to ask if I've deposited the sawbuck, and to check the bottom line of my bank book.

My mom's being worse than an asshole by pushing her husband to be even more prudishly offended than he already was by the game *her own goddamn parents taught me to play.*

Gramma Grace is the worst, though. She's the one trying to make me be pious and celibate every minute of every day of the year, with not even little vacations for girlfriends or poker or beer. Next time she brings up St. Stanislaus or celibacy, I'm asking her, *Even in high school and college?* Plus she won't be able to tell on me to my dad because the seminary plan's still a secret—unless she already blabbed to him. And even though nothing's about to happen with Laurie or Margie or anyone, I could also say, Why don't *you* try it?

3/12/18 The heavy sea has become raging. During the night one of the supply ships got off its course. HMS Leviathan returned and retrieved it.

At 4 p.m. all were once more in their original positions. Two soldiers from one of the transports were lost overboard.

To get one's meals has become amusing. Sitting on the deck doing one's best to juggle the food on the dishes furnishes more or less comedy. It recalls that adage, "There's many a slip twixt cup and the lip." No tables have been set since Monday. Life-belts were issued to everyone, as we are nearing the war zone.

3/13/18 As if trying to expose any "subs" that might be lying in wait, the sea has become raging again. Waves break over the sides. A blinding snowstorm screens us from our nearest convoy and howls its defiance at the "Tin fishes."

3/14/18 The Skipper stood an all night watch on the bridge, as we are in the war zone. Weather clear, and sea quite calm. A soldier from one of the transports was buried at sea.

Submarine was sighted by one of the munition ships. They fired two shots at it. Sub disappeared.

3/15/18 Weather was fair and warm. On account of being in the danger zone, no hammocks were given out. All hands off watch must sleep on the top deck. Rather chilly, with nothing over one but the firmament.

3/16/18 Six English destroyers appeared at about 8 a.m. to convoy us the balance of the way. Changed from 4 to 8, to 12 to 4 watch.

All hands must stay on the top side and look for "subs." The gun crews stand at the guns continually. Don't leave even for meals; they are brought to them. No hammocks issued.

3/17/18 Was quite tired after a sleepless night. Part of the night was spent watching phosphorus in the water, that appeared like so many twinkling stars. At times a large ball of fire would appear on the horizon.

The Hebrides appeared off our port side. Felt more relieved at the sight of land. Took all meals on the top side. Skipper is taking every precaution for the crew's safety, in the event we are hit.

No mention of St. Patrick's Day, even as they're cruising past Ireland? I guess because he and everyone else are scanning for subs. It also might've been dark as they passed the northern coast, which is where mostly Protestants lived.

At 1:30 p.m., we began to make 18 knots, for we are now at the particular part known as the "Ships' Graveyard." Continued at this rate of speed until 6 p.m., when we were inside the British "nets." Anchor was made about midnight off the town of Greenock.

3/18/18 Sunrise unveiled a very quaint town, situated at the foot of a chain of hills. The houses were covered with either thatched or red roofs.

At 1:30 p.m., we started up the Clyde River. The scenery was very beautiful. Highlands gave evidence of spring, as they appeared in the verdant hues. One in particular was conspicuous, for at its summit stood what appeared to be an ancient castle that would remind one of "Marmion" or "Lady of the Lake."

After proceeding for two hours, the clouds of smoke seemed to welcome us into the manufacturing centers. Soon we were amongst the large ship-building yards. They are said to be as great as any in Europe. They flanked both sides of the river, and the workers could be plainly seen, for at no point is it over 100 feet wide. The workmen paused in their efforts to defeat the Huns to wave a greeting.

Aeroplanes could be seen in the yard of the Albion Motor Car Co. Another place was making the much talked-about "Tanks." They were being tried out on ground especially prepared for them.

Whilst different workers came out to greet us, we were surprised to note that young women were amongst them. They were clad in khaki overalls.

And . . . ? Even in their overalls, how did they look?

Five o'clock was the time we finally got tied up to Prince's dock. A sigh of relief could be heard, for it was about 14 days and 3 hours since we had left N.Y.

The liberty "party" was called about 7:30 p.m. Before leaving the ship, the Captain gave a few instructions, also some startling news. A torpedo had passed near our bow on Sunday morning, and had missed the closest munition ship by about 20 feet. He also informed us that we were the first ship flying the Stars and Stripes that had entered this port in 3 years.

No sooner had we got ashore than we were facing more difficulty. We had nothing but the good American Dollars and their currency was English. Through the courtesy of the Y.M.C.A., we overcame this difficulty. People stopped, and in some cases started conversations to satisfy themselves that the "Yanks" had come. All seemed glad to see us.

Went to the movies after finding out, much to my disappointment, that a regular steak was beyond the question. Only lamb was offered, and sugar is never served in the Tea Rooms, as they call their eating emporiums.

3/19/18 Coaled ship. Twenty-one men came aboard. They were some of the survivors of an oil tanker that had been sunk.

Their first officer was taken prisoner. They claimed the "sub" was 260 feet long, and carried 4 four-inch guns.

Skipping ahead to 3/23/18, he writes, *Saturday night spent on liberty in Glasgow. Had an amusing evening watching the odd dances.*

That's *it?* Why can't he say *who* was dancing, and *where*, and with *whom*? And what the hell else happened? Did he dance with some Scotch women or just stand around watching? I know he didn't drink or play poker, though maybe he just didn't want to admit those things in his diary, knowing the fanatical stickler who'll read it someday. But he hadn't even met Gramma Grace yet. She was still Grace Lynch of New York, age seventeen. So weird to try to picture her then.

And now here's the week she asked me to focus on.

3/24/18 (Palm Sunday) All clocks were set ahead one hour last night, as specified by the Daylight Savings Committee. Went to St. Patrick's Church and attended 9 o'clock Mass. Received evergreen instead of palm.

Later visited Fr. Michael MacMahon, S.J. of St. Aloysius Parish, who put his hands on my shoulders and invited me to attend Tenebrae on Good Friday. His parish is quite old, but the church is rather new, having been dedicated in '08. The nave is nearly 50 feet wide, of re-enforced concrete, much resembling the inside of a barrel cut in half laterally, above the magnificent altar clad in gray marble.

3/25/18 Visited Botanic Gardens. Passed a pleasant hour amid splendid verdancy reflected in the many faceted mirrors within the glass and wrought iron structure of Kibble Palace, lifting my gaze above the nude marble sculpture of Eve.

3/26/18 Regular routine.

3/27/18 (Spy Wednesday) Went ashore. Attended Spy Wednesday services at St. Aloysius. Pleasant evening.

3/28/18 (Maundy Thursday) Regular routine.

3/29/18 (Good Friday) Attended Tenebrae at St. Aloysius. Received a host from Fr. MacMahon, S.J. Pleasant conversation with him afterward.

3/30/18 Captain's inspection. The first since September.

3/31/18 (Easter Sunday) Received mail from home, also a sweater from "Dixie."

Since Gramma always says *she* was his first girlfriend, Dixie must mean a naval charity in the South. If it was an actual girl's name, he wouldn't've used quotation marks. The key point is that he must've switched churches because the priest at St. Aloysius was Jesuit, but then comes the kicker: *Went to church in the morning and evening.* Two Masses in one day, both said by a Jesuit. You reading this, my little lamb? My celibate semen-husbanding seminarian?

Gramma's plan's pretty obvious. She gave me the diary to remind me it's time to tell my dad I want to become a Jesuit, even though the application to St. Stan's isn't due for ten months. She's obsessed. I can't even imagine how shocked she'll be if I told her I might not apply, though for sure she will switch on the waterworks. I'm still Catholic and all, but since I don't really want to be celibate, it's ixnay on her plan for me to get her out of Purgatory—though how many sins can the goddamn parish secretary possibly have on her soul?

The other reason she wants me to read *and probably memorize* these Holy Week entries is her war for my soul against the Hun Maddens. She's feeding me propaganda to turn me into a teetotaling Jebby. The Maddens want me to have fun, drink beer, play poker, go swimming with Margie, make out with Laurie or Margie, go to a regular college, get married, etc. The Maddens are Catholics, of course. They still go to confession and Mass on most Sundays. Gramma Betsy has holy cards and scapulars on top of her dresser. The difference is, she and Grampa aren't as fixated on it as Gramma Grace and my parents. I doubt the Maddens even care about Purgatory. When they die, they'll do their time there without complaining and get up to Heaven when they get there.

Whereas the fanatics I live with try to brainwash me pretty much every day of the year. They claim they hate Communists while using their same goddamn tactics. I'm only with the Maddens for part of the summer and maybe a few days at Thanksgiving or Christmas, yet the battle is really no contest: the Maddens are going to win. The other strange thing is, my mom is on the Killeens' side, against her own parents. My dad used to be sort of neutral but leaning toward his parents' side, especially on the subject of poker, though he's not against talking to girls, having kids, or drinking and smoking when you turn twenty-one.

Meanwhile, the only poker I ever play anymore, for chips worth a penny apiece, is with my St. Joan friends, though we did play one time with nickels and dimes, even quarters at the end, with Stan Krawczyk and two of his friends from St. Procopius. And I *still* won. Stan also plays at the Hinsdale Country Club caddy shack. You have to be fourteen to loop there. B caddies make $2.50 a bag; A's make $3.50, I think. Once you're big enough to carry doubles, you make eight or nine bucks a loop, depending on tips, almost twenty bucks a day if you go thirty-six holes on the weekends. That's why those guys can play stud for big money.

Grampa Vince didn't play poker, but no one should be making such a big effing deal about it. He put out fires, coaled and cleaned the boilers, helped lay mines in the sea to sink German subs. Sometimes they went off prematurely, killing his crew mates. It could've just as easily happened to him, in which case I wouldn't be here. The situation was easily dangerous enough that Gramma is right when she says he was a hero.

> *. . . Commenced mining at 5:15 a.m. At 5:35 a violent explosion was heard, followed by many others. We heard that the mines were exploding through some defects. We laid 180 and had two explosions. Was on watch in the engine room at the time. Felt an indescribable thrill when the first explosion occurred as I thought we were under fire. Expecting to meet a part of the German Navy at any time.*

Who *cares* if he didn't play poker?

I stay after on Tuesday to ask Miss Moore if I can write my civics report on the North Sea Mine Barrage instead of the branches of government. I know it's a long shot, but if I can get her to say yes I can kill these two birds with one stone.

The classroom gets quiet by 3:25, though it still smells of chalk and rotten bananas because it's too cold to open the windows. I erase the board and straighten the desks until Marybeth's questions get answered, which only takes like a day and a half. I recheck the chalk trays for spiders.

Miss Moore says she's never heard of the Barrage but seems pretty psyched when I tell her about it, especially when I say that my grandfather fought in it. "This is the one you were named after, right?"

"Yup." I'm surprised she remembered that.

"Sounds like a really cool project," she says, and I'm thinking, Great, till she adds, "but you still need to do the three branches. Too much of the state test is on them. You're gonna pass anyway, but we want you to pass it with flying colors. You know what I'm saying?"

"I guess."

She looks at me like, *What's this you* guess? If she hadn't let the detention slide last semester, I'd probably ask her again from a different angle, but she knows I'm aware that I owe her. Painfully effing aware. Plus I've made sure to not even come close to deserving another one.

"No no, you're right."

The good thing is, Miss Moore seems the same as before, pretty much, as long as I don't act like a wise guy. The only differences are, she probably has a boyfriend, and we still have this thing we're never supposed to bring up. I know she lives in Naperville, but her number's unlisted, so I haven't been able to find her address. There are too many Moores in the West Suburban phone book to tell if any of them might be her brother. And in the Chicago phone book, forget it. I obviously can't ask anyone to help me find out. Reid and Vogel and my other friends still can't believe I got away with having the lyrics. Krawdick says my dad or Gramma Grace must've helped get me off. Not as a criticism, though—as a compliment for getting away with it, but also for not ratting him out.

As I'm pulling on my coat, Miss Moore says, "What did he do on the *Baltimore*?"

"He mostly laid mines to booby-trap U-boats," I say, making sure *laid* and *booby* don't sound like double entendres. And since she's asking about *my* family, can't I ask if she has a brother? Something like, *Thought I heard your brother with the Corvette was in the Marines.* My palms are all clammy. "I never—me *or* my dad, not even my dad ever met him, though he's the one I'm named after."

"Ah." She tilts her head, smiles. "Did I know that already?"

"I—I dunno. Don't think so. Did you?" I think I might be standing too close to her, but when I take a step back my heel hits the leg of her desk in this weird way that knocks me off balance, like I got tackled from behind by a Chihuahua or something. To regain my balance I lurch too far forward.

"Whoa," she says, bracing my shoulder. "You okay?" Which of course is exactly when Ruth Ann marches in. They must both think I'm the biggest spaz pervert in history. I can't even talk to my teacher without toppling into her breasts?

"Fine, fine," I say, grinning like some huge clueless moron.

Ruth Ann just stands there, gray eyes wide open. Sometimes I wish she wasn't Reid's girlfriend, or Krawdick's. Anyway, I think Miss Moore smiles at her funny—like, *What is Duh's problem?*—before turning back to me. "Maybe you could do a second report, for some, you know, extra credit."

"Okay. Good idea. Hi, Ruth Ann."

"Hi," she says, making it sound like a question. "Should I go?"

"No, we're just about done here," Miss Moore says. To me she says, "Why doncha think about it? And only if you truly have time. Either way, keep studying those chapters, those handouts, even though I know you'll do fine . . ."

I rush out of the room, down the stairs, thinking about how her breasts felt against my collarbone and cheek, how much of a pitiful pervert I must've seemed to both of them, how Miss Moore had gasped and breathed in. My doozer's so hard I don't even want to kill myself anymore by the time I get onto the sidewalk.

In the spring of '18, Grampa Vince's penmanship got

harder to read for some reason, though I keep wishing he'd write longer entries in his sloppier cursive—sloppy because of the waves, I assume. I start skipping around more, looking for girlfriends or battle scenes.

4/5/18 Taken ill with a bad cold and threatened with diphtheria. Fourth case sent to the Hospital. Reports that fellows from the ship have a free-for-all with "Lime Juicers." A few injured on both sides.

4/6/18 Still confined to Sick Bay. British nurse says I might have diphtheria.

4/8/18 Allowed to leave Sick Bay after receiving a "shot" of antitoxin. Feel well, outside of a cold.

4/9/18 Received 184 mines aboard ship, of English make. The mines have seven horns and are to be set 35 feet below the surface.

4/10/18 The work of putting the horns on the mines progressing rapidly. They have an outer covering of lead to protect the glass containing acid, which when broken flows to the inner mechanism of the mine, causing the explosion.

4/11/18 The mines are now completed and ready to be dropped. This operation most likely shall be carried out tomorrow night. All hands quite anxious, owing to the fate of other ships that had been engaged in this hazardous work.

4/13/18 Started for our point of operation at 8:15 p.m. At 11:30 a submarine was seen on our course. This necessitated a change in course, resulting in a four-hour delay. One hundred eighty-one mines were laid between 3:55 and 4:41. Whilst steaming we averaged 16 knots. When planting we made 6 knots. When returning 3 shots were fired from the "H-6-Z," one of the British destroyers that was convoying us, at a sub. No further trouble. No one was allowed to sleep.

4/15/18 Received more mines. Engines overhauled. Received word that the "War Bayonet" was torpedoed.

4/16/18 Funeral of the 501 men from the "Lake Moore" that was caught by a sub in the Irish Sea on April 11.

4/21/18 Our third trip was made to try to stop the U-boat menace. 180 mines were placed in various places. We left earlier than usual for Greenock.

4/27/18 Planted 180 mines. We were escorted by a British zeppelin. It came so near the ship that the voices of the crew could be plainly heard. Its crew consisted of three men. After circling about for an hour, it disappeared.

5/1/18 Went ashore in a Recreation party for 5 ½ hours. Played baseball and defeated the U.S.S. Gold Sheep 9 to 7. I played second base and made two singles in four appearances. This is the first time since April 4th that I set foot on the old terra firma. This was part of a celebration of the 20th anniversary of the Baltimore running the gauntlet at Manila Bay, May 1st, 1898.

5/3/18 Pay day. Bought a $200.00 Bond. Received word that at least two explosions were noted in the fields we had planted, denoting the loss of two subs. Taking on coal, smashed middle finger of my left hand. Lost my gold ring.

Reid calls me about Saturday. His plan is to boost a six-pack from his dad's supply in their garage, drink it, then walk over behind Laurie's or Ruth Ann's, depending on whose house they're at. Maybe call first, or if her bedroom light's on toss BBs at the window. "Or *not* toss them, right? Just wait till we saw what we see."

"Count me in."

It's the first time it'll be only two of us: fewer guys to share the beers with, less likely to get pinched by the fuzz.

When I whisper into the phone that I might be able to pour some of my dad's gin into a jar and sneak it out under my jacket, he laughs. "You kidding me, man? Beer and *gin?*"

"Not *mixed*. Separately. Case we run outta beers. Which we're gonna."

"Wow, Duh. I mean—"

"What?" Last time we did this, we only had four beers to split between me, him, and Vogel. Plus he knows my dad hardly ever buys beer, so he always knows exactly how many he has.

"Jesus, Duh."

"Jesus what?"

He finally says, "Nothing. I'll see you tomorrow."

When I hang up in the kitchen, my mom says, "Who was that, at this hour?"

"Reid couldn't get one of the algebra problems." I don't know exactly what she's heard, but I can tell she doesn't believe me.

"Have you started either of those Dooley books?"

"Not yet," I say, walking out of the kitchen. "I'm savoring them till I finish my present from Grampa."

"Oh, right. So how is his diary then? Your dad says it's quite—"

"Grampa *Tom*."

6/26/18 Baseball game between the San Francisco and Baltimore. Baltimore 6 – Frisco 3. Today completes one year in the service. Commenced training at Newport, R.I. June 1917. Arrived aboard the Baltimore 8/22/17. First trip was to Hampton Roads for target practice. Up until December, most of the time was spent at New London. Left N.Y. 3/4/18 for European waters. In the past year had 15 days leave. Travelled approximately 8000 miles and visited 4 foreign ports.

6/29/18 Received word of American forces on the Western front.

7/2/18 Arrived at Invergordon at 10:30 a.m. Went ashore in the evening to give the town the once over. There are many restrictions as to where you may go, on account of large tanks that had not been forgotten by the camouflage artists.

7/4/18 Today, though far from the good old U.S.A., was spent in celebrating the 142nd anniversary of our Independence. It was an unusual celebration of this great day, for all Great Britain joined us. Here, at this port, the battleship Erin of his majesty's navy had the Stars and Stripes flying aside the Union Jack. The editorials of today's papers often and fiercely commented on the righteousness of the cause championed by the "Boys of '76."

At 1:30 the baseball team began playing, with myself batting second and playing second base. Our efforts resulted in a win for the Baltimore. The box score showed Baltimore 8 – Aroostook 1. I contributed one double and scored one run. Murray allowed but one hit.

Mr. Wilson would have wept if he saw the dinner that had been prepared for us. After dinner we were returned to the beach, the Empire Theatre being the objective, and a very good vaudeville and boxing program had been promised. The committee made good on this promise, for each number was a "howling" success. The bouts were four in number and consisted of 3 rounds each. Most of the party were in great "spirits" returning—mostly distilled.

After supper motion pictures were shown aboard ship and concluded the program of the day and left a feeling that on our 143rd anniversary of Independence, history shall have recorded our victory over the Kaiser, in our fight for world wide democracy.

8/8/18 Started out for a mining operation at 2:30 P.M. At 8:20 four depth bombs were dropped by British destroyers on a "sub," disabling her so she had to come to the surface. Trawlers then sunk her. A close call. Our convoy consisted of thirteen destroyers and four battleships, 10 minelayers, with 7000 mines.

8/9/18 Commenced mining at 8:30 A.M. More mines exploded than on our previous trips. At times as many as 25 would go up in rapid succession through a column of water that would rise and spread into three parts. It sometimes reached as high as two hundred feet. Every explosion would shake our ship from stem to stern. The rising water always preceded the sound of the explosion.

The depth bombs were dropped by H.M.S. Vampire and Observer off Mukee Skenny Lighthouse. Two prisoners taken. The U-boat had two 6" guns and four of smaller caliber.

Before midnight two torpedoes were fired at U.S.S. Aroostook. A sharp turn to the port side saved her. 380 mines exploded during operation.

8/17/18 Baltimore defeated Frisco 4-0. Murray allowed 2 hits and had 14 strikeouts. Crew won $3500.00 in wagers. . . .

9/6/18 Started on leave at 4 p.m. Arrived at Edinburgh 11:30 p.m. Staying in Temperance Hotel.

9/7/18 Went to Braid Hill in the morning. Left Edinburgh at 1:08 p.m. and arrived at Inverness at 9 p.m. Put up at Temperance Hotel for the night.

9/8/18 Got back to the ship at noon. The whole trip was a succession of enjoyments. Ship was coaled whilst I was away.

Whilst passing her table in the lunchroom on Wednesday, I stop to ask Laurie about the algebra homework. From her tooth marks in the bread, I can tell she's taken exactly one bite of her sandwich. "Was it the evens or odds on page eighty-six?" I ask her. "I forgot to write it down."

When she finishes swallowing, she says, "Evens."

"Did either of your grandfathers fight in World War One?" I ask, since it might be easier to get her to say yes for a date if we had something in common to talk about.

I can tell she's surprised by the question, but before she can answer, Marybeth says, "What's that got to do with the algebra?"

Laurie blushes. "I think my mom's dad was in the Red Cross . . ."

"My dad's dad was in the navy," I say. I obviously can't ask her out *here*, can't even ask if it's okay to call her. When I finally do call her, if her effing old man finally doesn't answer, we can continue the war conversation. Even if old man Langan does answer again, I won't have to hang up. I can just say, May I please speak to Laurie? It's about World War One.

"So, anyway, thanks. Just the evens," I say, heading toward my regular table. "That's what I thought."

That night I skip ahead to the last of the entries. During the middle of September, he wrote "Regular routine" almost every day, except for *9/13/18 Shawmut defeated Baltimore 14-10. News of U.S. Army's success at St. Michel under Gen. Pershing.* After that he starts hearing rumors that the war will be over soon.

9/21/18 Another submarine was sighted at 11:45 p.m. All ships made a smoke screen. The Vampire dropped depth charges. Thick oil was seen later on the surface, and possibly the sub was destroyed. Later two German bodies were found. Anchored at 6 p.m. at Invergordon.

9/22/18 Rear Admiral Belknap came aboard and informed us of the important work we had done during the past six months. He also confirmed the report as being true of going to the States, and wished us all a very pleasant and safe voyage.

Preparations are made to coal the ship.

9/26/18 Up at 4 a.m. Underway at 8:11 a.m. for the States. Accompanied the rest of the Mine Force as they were going out on another "Excursion." All the ships sent signals wishing us a safe voyage etc. Whilst sending one of the signals one of the men fell overboard and was drowned.

We anchored at Scapa Flow at 4:36 p.m.

9/27/1 Standing by to continue our trip. Our battleships had antiaircraft practice at 9:30 p.m. Clock was pushed back an hour. Received word that a German battle cruiser was sunk in a mine field in the North Sea.

9/28/18 Have the 12 to 4 watch for this week. Underway at 6:03 p.m., accompanied by two British destroyers. At about 9:30 a.m. we passed a mountainous coast. All of the mountains were snow capped. Sea rough.

9/29/18 Speeding along at 13½ knots per hour. At noon we were 3727 miles from Cape Henry Lighthouse. Weather clear. Sea calm.

9/30/18 At 1:00 a.m., I saw the Northern Lights; they were very brilliant until about 1:45 a.m.

10/1/18 Sea still running high. Had to slow down to 10 knots. At noon we were 2956 miles from Cape Henry.

10/3/18 Sea was very rough. So far it has been a miserable trip. One man was knocked out by falling on the main deck, when a wave came over the side. All meals are eaten off the deck. Now 2402 miles from Cape Henry.

10/4/18 Had to slow down to 10 knots on account of rough seas. We are using only six boilers—two being out of commission.

10/6/18 Received word that three U-boats were in the vicinity, and to be ready to make all possible speed at a moment's notice.

10/7/18 Changed our course and are making for Halifax, as we must have coal. All hands were up at 5 a.m. to man the port and starboard rails and keep a sharp lookout for subs. Had 3 hours sleep in 24.

10/8/18 All hands up at 5 a.m., the same as yesterday. We are 496 miles from Halifax. Passed an iceberg at 2 a.m.

10/9/18 Speeded up to 13½ knots. The weather is clear and the sea calm. 'Tis about the best day we have had since leaving the States.

10/10/18 Tied up to a dock in Halifax at 8:26 a.m. and commenced coaling at 9:10 a.m. Saw many wounded soldiers borne on stretchers off a hospital ship. The U.S. destroyer Wilcox is also in port.

10/11/18 Underway at 4:04 p.m. for the States, the Captain having received orders to proceed to New York. Everyone was much pleased with the news. We are making 14 knots. Weather clear, sea very calm.

10/13/18 Sighted Ambrose Channel lighthouse at 11:07 a.m. Passed a convoy of six British transports, two destroyers and two American cruisers carrying our troops "over there." Anchored at Tompkinsville on Staten Island at 2 p.m. The first liberty party went ashore at 3:15 p.m. Notice was posted that we shall be allowed to wear a gold chevron for our services in the war zone.

Finished my day's work at 8:30 p.m. Been up since 3:30 a.m.

Finis

The rest of the pages, more than half of the notebook, are blank. No girlfriend in Scotland, no girlfriend he's going home to, since Gramma says they didn't meet until 1922. But maybe he'll kiss someone else on Staten Island, like that sailor did in Times Square on VJ Day.

I really like the way he played a solid second-base for the *Baltimore* team, which seems to have won at about a .750 clip while in Scotland, good enough to win any pennant race. He never brags, but he must've been pretty damn good. I wish we could've played catch a few times, maybe even traded gloves for a while. If he was a good fielder with his old flat and stiff one, he'd make about an error a year with an A2100. I wish I could ask him about some of the things he didn't do, or did but decided not to put in his diary.

I wish my dad had been able to play catch with him, or talk to him about politics. Like about how to handle the Soviets.

Even if I don't write the report for extra credit, when Gramma asks what I think, I can say what a brave sailor and staunch Catholic he was. What a *really* staunch Catholic. I can say he reminds me of Nellie Fox, who she knows is my favorite player, even after we traded him to the Astros.

It's obvious from the Holy Week entries that Grampa Vince would agree with his future wife's plan to push their first grandson to become a priest, not to mention stopping him from playing poker and drinking. If he were still alive, the battle between the Killeens and the Maddens might've tipped in the other direction. Who knows? Even though if it was up to the Killeens and my mom, I'd spend the rest of my life in a temperance rectory, saying four Masses a day, with my fingers all sappy from passing out evergreen sprigs.

I obviously can't tell Gramma her husband was sort of a stick in the mud, at least compared to Grampa Tom. I can't even talk to Ellen about it. I know she'd agree his devoutness was weird, but she won't read the diary now because she's mad Gramma gave it to me instead of her. It doesn't matter to Smellen that it was only because I was named for its author and might join the navy someday, or that Gramma's wedding ring is a thousand times more valuable—or that she gets to get married after college and maybe have a few boyfriends in the meantime, even if they aren't John Lennon. But as soon as I brought it up she'd start in about how Catholics favor men over women, nuns can't set foot on the altar, etc. etc. etc. Our dad might even agree with her, on some points at least.

As if she liked nuns in the first place! And how is it my fault what the rules of the Church are, or that she can't be a sailor or priest?

But all of a sudden I know how to settle this argument. For her birthday, she got a four-speed amplified stereo hi-fi. For mine, I got this old diary. All I have to say is, *Let's trade then.*

Just before dinner on Holy Thursday—or Maundy Thursday, as Gramma still calls it—my dad's getting ready to show off the Last Supper sculpture he bought as a Lenten Offering to his family, though it's also to impress Fr. Ted next time he swings by for dinner. He's already hung it in the dining room where the Killeen coat of arms used to be. The lion surrounded by three three-leafed clovers is going back above his dresser, I think.

The apostles, the table, the background, and the big swanky frame are all cast in bronze but polished to look more like gold. Only one apostle pops far enough out that you can see around his whole head. You can see only the front and one side of the other heads, plus the folds in the robes, the curls in the beards and long hair. A few of them seem to be arguing, and St. James the Greater is shaking his index finger to help make his point. Judas's nose makes him look Jewish, plus he has that scheming look in his eye. Jesus looks peaceful but sad; he already knows Judas has betrayed him and what's about to happen in the Garden of Gethsemane as soon as they're done eating; He even knows what'll happen tomorrow. His hair's the longest, of course. Anything this modernistic can't show his halo, so you have to use faith to imagine it.

"But so how're they all on one side?" Ellen asks. "Unless they're posing for wall sculptures in 33 A.D. there'd be six on each side, with humble J.C. at the foot."

Our dad mustn't have heard her, but Gramma sure did. "J. *C.*?" she says.

"Someone's *mouth* will be washed out with *soap,*" says our mom.

"It's art, sacred art," says our dad, using his cigarette hand to thumb up the lower right corner maybe a twelfth of an inch. He steps back to see if it's level. "That about right?"

Ellen shakes her head but says nothing. Neither do I or the littler kids. Our mom keeps on glaring at Ellen. "Oh, honey," says Gramma. "It's perfect."

"Plus even people who don't believe in God," I say, "have to admit his son was a pretty decent guy all around."

"Decent 'guy'?" says my dad, as my mom says, "*Who*

doesn't believe in Him?"

"No one I know," I say, to keep them from exploding. It works.

We're at opposite ends of the table, but I think I also hear them say the sculpture cost a hundred bucks. Gramma definitely says something like we got a good deal on it because she works in the rectory. "And no tax," she says now.

Still ogling the sculpture while she spreads on some tartar sauce, my mom says, "I'll bet it's practically good enough to hang in the Vatican."

The three adults bob their heads, no surprise. Anything to do with religion they automatically agree on. The thing is, what she said was, "I'll bet." It just came so natural, she didn't even notice she said it. But betting's the last thing on earth she'd ever think of actually doing, not even if the Communists came and tried forcing her to. Not even if they gave her the money to bet with, so she couldn't lose a red cent. It's the principle, she'd tell them, fingering her olive-wood rosary, which for some reason they've forgotten to confiscate. Good Roman Catholics don't gamble, she'd say, all proud and confident. That would be that. Chinese water torture, Russian roulette, forced to smoke Cuban cigars—nothing could make her toss in one chip. She'd rather risk shooting herself in the temple than bet fifteen cents with four aces.

My dad is like both of his parents, staunch Catholic verging on Holy Roller, even though he was raised by only one of them, whereas my mom's almost the opposite of hers, even though both of them raised her. It's like the square root of negative one in our weird family algebra.

Ellen and I are mixes of both sets of grandparents, which is probably why we disagree more and more with our parents. The younger kids are To Be Determined, plus my mom's not done having them yet.

"Pass the salt, please," she says, and I pass it. She knows I'm still pissed that they've garnished my two favorite presents. She'd probably admit to herself that it's clearly unfair, but it's not the kind of thing she'd back down on. As we look at each other, her eyes say, *When did our sweet little altar boy turn into this devil who talks back and gambles?* Mine say, *Yeah, sure, I'll obey you, I love you and all, but don't think it means that I like you.*

After finishing most of my homework I try to call Laurie, yanking the upstairs receiver around the corner and into the bathroom, but when her old man answers on the second ring I have to rush back out to hang up. It's the third time I've done it, and I've heard they can get the phone company to trace it after a certain number of hang-ups. Like three. So now I'll have to talk to her at school again, or on the way home, and wait at least a year before I try calling again.

I pour myself some chocolate milk and sit in my usual place at the table. Everything's been cleared except an ashtray and the paper. Dear Abby, What should

I do if my girlfriend's creepy plumber old man keeps answering the phone? Dear Hanger-Upper, Maybe try calling her after school but before plumbers get home from work, like around a quarter to five. Dear Abby, Hey, good idea, but what if she's not even my girlfriend? Dear Horny Pity, How hard can it be to get the Colarcos' number from long-distance directory assistance?

The photo of President Kennedy still has the black sash draped across the middle. Whenever it starts drooping, Gramma trips over herself in a rush to retape it. She says it stays up till November 22 at the soonest, because that's how long the Killeens will officially be in mourning, whatever the newspapers say.

Ever since he was assassinated, she's become even more of a stickler about anything having to do with him. Just last week, when Kevin asked when we were getting a picture of President Johnson, she said, "Instead?"

"No, different," he said. "Of the *new* president." He must've thought that because we've had a picture of Kennedy on our wall for four years, half his entire life, we'd always have a picture of whoever's the president hanging there. Like our house was the post office or something. But here's where things really got strange.

"No, we most certainly will not," Gramma told him, not smiling at all. Almost as if Gramma Betsy was talking. Gramma Grace always explained things, *gently* explained things, usually to within an inch of their life when a little kid asked her a question, but this time she was still too angry about everything that happened in

Dallas to say anything positive, especially about someone from Texas. It was almost like she wanted President Johnson to be assassinated too, as a kind of retaliation for what Oswald and Ruby did, even better if the trigger got pulled by a Texan *in Texas,* and so on and so on till everyone in Texas was dead. Not that she'd light candles or offer novenas for that to happen, but I'd bet a million bucks she wishes it would, at least in that place in her mind she keeps secret even from Jesus. And according to her, she and my parents might be voting for Rockefeller this time—news Gramma Betsy of course would be thrilled with.

"How come?" Kevin said.

Once he or Sheila or Brian or Colleen gets going with the questions, wild zebras can't stop them. I could see Gramma fretting to think of a nice way to explain to him how she felt about Johnson—about all Southerners, really—but even after standing up, patting the top of Kevin's head, lighting a cigarette and staring into space for ten seconds, all she came up with was, "Because that is never going to happen."

I thought he was going to cry. "Never *ever?*"

She shook her head, nodded. She could've easily said something to soften it, like, *You'll understand certain things when you're older now, deah*, or *President Johnson never served on the altar, like you are about to if you keep listening to your big brother*, but she was just too mad that anyone had dared to even suggest we hang up a picture of Johnson, let alone take down the one of Kennedy, or even the sash, to give her cute little grandson an ungrouchy answer. He looked over at me, confused but not crying yet. When I gave him an it's-up-to-our-weird-crazy-Gramma shrug, it just seemed to make him more scared. And then it was *Gramma* who looked like she was going to cry, like she might even have a nervous breakdown or something. Like you couldn't rule out that she'd blurt, *Oh, God damn you!* But all she did was pick up her matches and Kents, pat his head with them, and stalk through the kitchen and down the back stairs to her room.

Oh. My. *God!*

"Why was Gramma so grouchy?" he finally said. No tears rolling down, but his eyeballs were glistening.

"It's complicated, buddy. I think it's because her two favorite men are both dead. Besides Dad, of course."

"*Two* favorite? Who?"

"President Kennedy and Grampa Vince. Where you been, kid?"

He scrunched up his face while he thought about that. "They're both up in heaven, right?"

"Of course. But that's not the point."

"What about Uncle Don?"

"Hmm, yeah, you're right." Uncle Don won't be going to heaven, but I couldn't say that to his eight-year-old nephew. "Forgot about him." I also couldn't say he's not one of Gramma's top favorites because he's a drinker, or because he and Aunt Blair might be getting divorced. I just said, "Besides him and Dad."

"Plus you're a man too."

I fake-punched his shoulder. "Not when you're twelve, bud."

"You're almost thirteen, though. Next week."

"Yeah, but even when you're thirteen, you still have a few years to go."

"What, like seven or eight?"

I nodded. "In eight it's official, because you turn twenty-one."

"What're you gonna be then, ya think?"

"Not positive yet, but probably a chaplain, a sailor, marine, baseball or football player if I'm good enough. Or maybe a businessman."

"You're already good enough as an end."

"To play in the pros?" I shook my head, snorted. "You kidding?"

He thought about that, squirming like he needed to pee. "Daddy's a businessman."

"A businessman who used to be a sailor, just like Grampa Vince. President Kennedy's dad was a businessman too."

He stared at the photo. "But so when do ya gotta decide by?"

"Pretty soon, man. Pretty damn soon."

He nodded, all serious. You could tell he was proud I'd said *damn* right in front of him, plus neither of us made a big deal of it. To him it would prove he wasn't a kid anymore: he'd made his Communion, he didn't cry when Gramma got grouchy with him, people said swear words in front of him. He was also about to start serving. That's when I realized he was already a year older than I'd been when I started. For some reason Gramma hadn't gotten him started yet. Maybe because he was still learning the Latin responses, or the Pope hadn't decided yet whether American Masses should be said in English from now on.

He kept asking questions, and I kept trying to answer them in ways he could relate to, which was doubly weird because usually Gramma was the sweet, patient one and Ellen and I were the ones too busy to talk to the littler kids. He wanted to know whether you got more homework in fifth than in fourth. The Beatles stink, right? Who'd ever want to hang out with *girls*? Is bluffing the same thing as lying? In the meantime our mom was yelling down from upstairs that it was time for him to put on his PJs. "You too, Vince. It's past nine o'clock on a school night."

After we both yelled, "Okay!" Kevin whispered, "But can you teach me to play when Lent's over?"

Oh boy. This was the third or fourth time he'd asked me to, though never during Lent after he knew I gave it up, though teaching *was* different from playing. "Maybe if you're with us in Mahopac," I said, "when Mom and Dad aren't there."

"Like this summer, you mean?"

The first time I'd stayed there without any other Killeens, I was eleven and the cottage wasn't even finished, though our parents might want Kevin to wait till he's eleven too, since they'd heard about the poker and beer and Uncle Thomas's shenanigans, though I didn't think they'd heard about Margie. The cottage had bathrooms and walls now, so more of us could stay there, and we wouldn't have to crap in the woods. "Just ask 'em," I said. "Better if you ask than me. It'd be cool if we flew on the plane together."

His big eyes lit up, before he squinted and got serious again. "Plus I swore not to tell, right?"

"About me teaching you how to play?"

He slid off his chair but kept squirming while he stood there in front of me. After looking around to make sure no one could see or hear us, he nodded.

"Jeez, buddy, let's hope so. Otherwise—"

"Cross my heart, hope to die, stack of Bibles," he said, crossing himself in a rush then reaching up on tiptoe as far as he could, to show me how high the stack was he was swearing on.

"Deal."

Kings Up

Cursing and muttering, Swede slammed the screen door behind him. His hair was beaded with raindrops from waiting at the first tee for his members to finally decide it was drizzling too hard to play. "Dildo fruits think they can *stiff* me?" He viciously shrugged off his jacket. "Stiff *me?*" He stepped over the bench of the picnic table and shouldered his way into the space across from mine, between Tennessee and Vogel. Vogel had to slide over quick.

"Ain't that their job?" asked Tennessee, reluctantly scooching in the other direction. "Just don't let Stan hear ya say it."

"Fuck them, fuck Stan, and fuck you," Swede said matter-of-factly.

Tennessee stared at him, jutting his stubbly chin. "Your *what* hurts?"

"Hey, language!" Stan yelled from his office, though we all knew he wouldn't really do anything. He never came out except to take a leak or lock up. He had gray hair, crooked black bifocals, and always seemed kind of exhausted. When he didn't have loops to assign, he stayed behind his desk marking Hawthorn forms or talking on the phone to his bookie. He let Charlie Rupp, his assistant, do most of the work. Charlie lived two blocks away with his parents but drove his red fastback Mustang to the shack every day and parked it next to Stan's beater Stude.

"Yeah yeah . . ." Swede was calmer by now. "But definitely not 'yeah-yeah-yeah.' Them longhair English fruits're even worse."

Tennessee hollered, "Got it, Mr. Caddy Master, sir!" He and Stan were old buddies—they headed down to Hialeah to follow the ponies each winter—though no one got a loop if Stan had a beef with him. But what did Tennessee care if Stan was pissed off at Swede? Some things made sense around here, and some didn't.

Tennessee said something else under his breath, and Swede jumped back up, but it was just to pull his wallet from his jeans. After plucking out a half dozen sawbucks and fins, he sat down again, flattening the bills on the table. "*Andale,*" he said. "Let's play some high draw."

We were already playing it. What he meant was, things would change now that *he* had sat down. The price of poker was going way up in a hurry. I'd been waiting for this to happen for a couple three weeks, though I wasn't quite ready to pull out the rest of my wad yet.

Vogel opened the next hand for seventy-five. Tom Zrout, the dealer, said, "Pasadena." Even with jacks, I passed too, because I knew what was coming. Tom Cziesla, an A-jock from Downers Grove North who was growing a scraggly beard, also passed. After Tennessee called, Swede raised without looking at his cards, staring at Vogel's right sideburn to make a point of not looking. "*Two* seventy-five," he said, snapping the ends of a wrinkly fin. He laid it across the pot, started picking out change. His hands were so big, you couldn't tell if he took exactly $2.25 in change. His attitude was, why would I palm quarters when I've got forty bucks on the table, plenty more in my wallet, and I never fail to hammer you dipshits? We'd all heard him say the only reason he caddied at all was, if he didn't, he couldn't play the course on Mondays or take our money here in the shack. CADDIES ONLY.

I was pretty surprised when Vogel called the re-raise, since he liked to fold trouble hands or push all his money in with trips or better. But I wasn't surprised when Tennessee called. Maybe he had a made hand, and he certainly liked the pot's price, but he also knew Swede a lot better than we did, on top of being plain batshit loco himself. He combed his greasy hair straight back behind his ears so the stringy ends reached past his collar—more like a jailbird's than a beatnik's, though not near as long as a hippie's. None of us B-jocks knew his real name. He was supposedly from Holler, Tennessee, and didn't dig the name his parents gave him.

I doubted he'd even been baptized. He was gnarled-up and ropy, but calling himself Tennessee was kind of like a fat guy named Rudolf calling himself "Minnesota Fats" to come off as more of a badass.

And what do you know if Vogel didn't draw *three*? I'd been playing with him since fifth grade, and even in those penny-ante games he was tighter than St. Scholastica's twat. He'd avoided this game because you could lose your whole wad in one hand, and now he's calling Swede's raise with one pair?

Flipping his discard at Zrout, Tennessee said, "Gimme a heart," then shuffled the new one in with his keepers. Swede tapped his cards to stand pat. He loved playing draw because he could make every hand five-card chicken. He and Tennessee hated stud because the four exposed cards made it harder to bluff or finesse you, plus you had to remember every card folded. Too much like work, Swede would say. And forget dealer's choice. They'd tell you to start your own game if you asked to play anything but five-draw, jacks-or-better, for table stakes. It was way way way hairier than our limit games, if not quite as bad as the open-stakes action Yardley talked about in *The Education*, where you could wait for four aces and bet all you had in the bank, or the deed to some farm. Table stakes meant you could only bet whatever cash you had on the table before the hand started.

Vogel led out with a fin, so he must've improved. He sounded pretty proud of himself croaking "Five all day," but he didn't look happy when Tennessee raised it up to $18.65, all he had left. Swede took a drag on his Lucky and tapped off some ash, blowing a smoke ring that wobbled out over the pot. That Tennessee was loco enough to push in with anything didn't keep him from hitting his fair share of draws. Swede tilted his loose tooth again, then amazed me by folding.

As Vogel peeked at his hand again, he blushed a shade pinker than his sunburn. As usual, his pugschnoz was peeling. He winced. He'd either forgotten to maintain his poker face or decided it made the same difference once Tennessee bet all his bread. Vogel only had about thirteen bucks left, with over thirty sitting there in the pot, but every extra second he studied his hand, Tennessee got twice as confident. "John the Baptist only gots a pair . . ."

"Altar boy folds, though," said Swede, "he sure as shit better show openers."

"I know the damn rules," Vogel said. "No talking if you're not in the hand."

Instead of cold-cocking him with an overhand right to the temple, Swede leaned back and stretched. "Where's Roscoe?"

Tennessee shrugged. "Language, language," he said, mocking Vogel.

I knew Vogel knew Tennessee had been a 5-to-1 dog to hit a flush, assuming he'd stayed with four hearts, which he probably hadn't. Plus he knew how much the pro caddies loved to whipsaw us out of "their" pots.

We'd even talked about the possibility they worked as a team—Tennessee, Roscoe, and Swede—showing each other their cards, sending signals and whatnot. But the pot was so big now, times the odds Tennessee would be bluffing, Vogel pretty much had to call.

But he didn't. He flipped up red queens, mucked his others. Tennessee pushed all five of his face down into the muck pile, helping Zrout swirl it around.

"Fold them four titties," said Swede, "for all the no-good they can do ya."

Tennessee raked in the pot. "Only four he ever seed," he said, cackling.

"I seen plenty, don't worry," said Vogel. We both knew that was a whopper, but it was good to see him sticking up for himself, and for us. His face was even redder than it had been a minute ago, either because they were pissing in his Cheerios about getting to second base, or he'd made up his mind that Tennessee bluffed him. Or both. He tried to smile cockily but just couldn't quite pull it off.

"Prolly ever *will* see," said Swede.

The best weather for poker was this on-and-off drizzle, nothing hard or steady enough to make them close the course. Even on sunny days, B-jocks sometimes didn't get out till eleven or noon, so we couldn't make more than one loop. While waiting we played penny-a-point hearts or nickel-ante stud on pushed-together Nehi crates. We only got to use the picnic table when the pros and A-jocks were out. Grotty with butt burns and carved-in initials, the top was usually covered with a red checkered cloth so our money or cards wouldn't fall through the slats.

Most of us had either just graduated or were already in high school. Only a couple of guys were in college. Roscoe and Tennessee were both around forty, by far the oldest guys I'd ever met who weren't married or priests. Tennessee had two missing teeth. More than two maybe, since you couldn't see back to his molars.

We all knew Swede was thirty-three, since he'd announced it was time for him to found his own religion. He'd also said if he didn't make so much playing draw, he'd become a pro golfer. "I'm talking the tour, man, not no faggot givin' lessons to dingleberries." According to Zrout, Swede played scratch, even in ten-dollar Nassaus with local club pros. Vogel said he'd shot 67 from the black tees two Mondays ago—Swede had, not Vogel. When I reminded him that he'd never played a single hole with Swede, let alone eighteen, he said, "Even Stan admits he could break eighty easy with just his 5-iron and putter, if he needed to."

"Needed to?" I said. "Why'd he 'need' to?"

"Duh-uh. To win some massive wager, duh-umbshit."

"Oh, is that why he needed to, PAM?"

"Why, yes, Duh, it is."

I'd showed him both middle fingers, and he showed me his. We argued about everything, from the words to songs to whether Lucinda Pilarski wore falsies, even though our parents carpooled us here, with the Zrouts. We used to call Vogel Pan because his face was as round as a frying pan, but now we called him what you sprayed onto a pan so pancakes and sausages wouldn't stick to it. That was really all he'd seen "plenty" of.

I lit up a Lucky and inhaled without coughing. The first one of the day made me dizzy, probably because I'd been practicing on Gramma's Kents. I could usually handle Camels and Luckies if I didn't pull too hard, or they didn't get hotboxed while we shared one after school. Luckies were the coolest because they were toasted, but also because the red target showed through your pocket. L.S./M.F.T. didn't *officially* stand for Let's Screw/My Finger's Tired, but still. They were too strong for most chicks and ladies, but it was only a rumor they didn't smoke them because Loose Straps/Mean Floppy Tits, though it kind of made sense in a way, for moms and especially grammas. Nuns were forbidden by Cardinal Meyer to smoke *any* brand, though a few of the younger ones, like Sr. Janet, still snuck them sometimes. Kents were for ladies and sissies, especially when the Micronite filters got smudged with pink lipstick.

When I finally peeked in at trip deuces I opened for a buck, and Swede was the only guy who called. I drew two. Trying to intimidate me with the eight straight or nine flush cards he could yank out his ass, Swede drew just one, hoping I'd forget the other thirty-nine or thirty-eight that left him with diddly-squat.

To make it easier to look at my cards, I stubbed out my Lucky in the saucer we used as an ashtray. My replacements turned out to be jacks. Well well well. "Czechoslovakia," I said. Even though I knew he gave me credit for trips, I was sandbagging, knowing he'd bet. Because I knew that he knew that *I* knew the odds against my hitting a full house were 15 to 1. When he pushed out $2.75, I waited for maybe twelve seconds before jacking it up. "Seven straight."

"Was hoping you'd do that," he said. "Catlick-school boy make a fullie?" He tilted the tooth. He wanted to scare me, but not into silence. He wanted to hear how confident I sounded. Not answering him while maintaining my poker face was fifty times harder than when Vogel or Uncle Thomas tried staring me down.

"We know he's too chicken to bluff me, unless . . ."

I looked from his mouth to the dripping spruce through the window screen behind him. "Less what?" Tennessee asked him. They kept glaring at me while they talked to each other—but mostly, I realized, to me.

"Less he got lucky," said Swede.

"Which in which case he wouldn't *be* bluffing . . ."

"Less he's got a gold horseshoe lodged up his ass . . ."

"Which maybe he just likes the feel of . . ."

"No maybes 'bout that . . ."

Without the balls to come out and say it, Vogel still had enough to clear his throat, saying without words that they shouldn't be discussing my hand with each other. I raised my eyebrows and bobbed my head to show I agreed, though with all their talking and stalling, I figured the best Swede could have was a flush. What I couldn't tell was whether their kibitzing made him less or more likely to call. But even if the answer was less, there was no way to make them shut up.

"Twerp's twelve to one not to hit quads or fill up . . ."

"Thass right," said Tennessee, squinting at the backs of Swede's cards. "Assumin' you can beat bitty pairs . . ."

"Bitty pairs, huh? I can iron out his three lonesome cowboys all nice and dandy for him. Just decidin' how much I should *raise* . . ." I don't know what my face did, but my scalp and forearms crinkled with voltage. Had he hit some bullshit miracle straight flush on me, or a bigger full house? "How much you got left?"

"Twenty-four eighty-five," I said right away.

He nodded, kept staring and thinking. I thought he was going to call, but I wasn't really shocked when he finally passed. What shocked me and most everyone else was the ace-high straight he rolled over. Tennessee made a production of gasping and bugging his eyeballs. "Whoa, *daddy*!"

Zrout whistled. "Folds *Broadway*?"

When Tennessee demanded to see my openers, I showed him the jacks.

"Thass *it?*"

Mucking the deuces face down, I shrugged nonchalantly. I could've shown them all five, to cement the idea that when they drew one on me, I only raised after the draw with hands that beat flushes and straights. The jacks might've looked like a bluff, but I sort of meant it more as a taunt.

Swede was able to buy four of the next six "bitty" pots, mostly on the strength of his nobody-pushes-*me*-around front, but it only made the fact that I'd taunted *or* bluffed him more perfect. He wasn't going to forget that the next time we played a big hand. I also felt slightly less chicken when I reminded myself his real name was—get this—Jerker Hansen. It was supposed to be pronounced *Yerker*, but nobody had the *cojones* to call him that, with a J *or* a Y. Even if he wasn't a poker player, he obviously needed a nickname.

Guys who went to St. Joan or St. Procopius didn't usually get them, at least not cool ones that stuck, like "Minnesota" or "Doc" or "Wild Bill." We got named after saints and that was the end of the story. St. Vincent de Paul, St. James the Lesser, St. Francis was a sissy, etc. Sault St. Marie, before she sues you. Vogel's favorite was St. Basilissa, patron saint of breasts, expose them and pray for our sins. Obviously no one was about to start calling me "Bronx" or "Illinois" or, worse, "Lisle." That would be as bad as Yardley's "Old Adhesive," though no one really called him that. It was almost always "Herbert O. Yardley."

Anyway, as the drizzle kept the game from breaking up, I kept following his advice about only calling Swede's or Tennessee's openers with aces up or better. I should've played *more* hands against them, not less, but I reversed it to give myself fewer tough decisions. If you didn't improve on the draw, it was next to impossible to get either, let alone both, of them to lay down their hand, and one of them usually bet all he had. Vogel knew I was studying Yardley, but for obvious reasons I hadn't told anyone else at the shack.

Swede kept checking pre-draw with his busts and made hands, then raising whoever opened in front of him. About a third of the time he didn't even look at his cards. If his raise got called, he'd stand pat or draw one, and go, "Let's bump it up all the way." Sometimes he'd slap down his wad, other times gently lay it on the pot, like a host onto a tongue, then tap it with the yellow nails of his smoking fingers. "Just feels better *in*." After everyone passed, he'd turn over busts like 3-6-7-8-9, to get us to call him more often. But even with trips, how were you supposed to call fifty bucks, or even twelve or thirteen if that was all you were playing? Sometimes, of course, he'd get called, usually by Cziesla or Tennessee, but it never made him dial down his flamethrower. Plus he always made sure to have the biggest wad on the table. I didn't even think moving his tooth was a tell anymore, since I'd seen him do it before showing down monsters *and* bluffs.

But all this did was make me want to bust him even more. The trick was deciding which hands to call with pre-draw. Yardley says to raise the opener or open yourself with queens up or better, but fold to a raise with two smaller pairs, since you're eleven-to-one not to fill up. He says to draw three to a pair against two or more players, though in this game you were usually heads-up with Swede. I planned to draw two with big trips but sometimes disguise them by taking just one.

You could buy a new Schwinn with a few of these pots, but what I really wanted now was a car, even if I wouldn't turn sixteen for twenty-one months. That's why I'd started bringing my Federal Reserve Wad to the shack every day: a hundred and twenty-five bucks. If I could find some good spots and my timing was right, there was a half-decent chance I could triple it. What I needed to do was stop pussyfooting around. Since it had to be on the table to do me any good, I finally leaned back and slid my hand down into my left front shorts pocket.

Vogel's eyes bugged when he saw it, though I'd promised him for weeks I would do this. "Duh's lost his marbles. Might lose more than his marbles."

"Wouldja lookee here now?" said Swede. "The kid's playing—how much?"

I fanned out the bills. "One fifty-eight and some change now."

Guys started edging their soda crates forward or standing a foot or two closer. "There goes *that* roll," one said. Even if anyone was rooting for me, he wouldn't have the balls to do it out loud. I wouldn't've either. In poker, you were all on your own. As I passed the next seven hands in a row, it began to sink in that waiting for trips could cost me way more than whatever I'd make when I hit them.

On his own next deal, Swede made his usual raise. After Vogel and Zrout passed, I went against Yardley by calling with the 3-4-9-ace of diamonds. Cziesla and Tennessee passed. Swede drew two, advertising trips. I drew one. Without looking at his replacements, he bet a wrinkled sawbuck. "Nothin's wild now, remember. Maybe when you're playin' with nuns and cripples. Not here."

I squeezed out my hand. No fifth diamond, but it could've been worse: ace of clubs. "Who said anything about wild cards?"

"Not you, huh? Not the guy bettin' on the come first time this decade?"

"Ah-ah. Not me."

"Ya just *look* like ya need one, I guess." He stared me down as I shook my head no. Unfortunately, when I took a swig of Coke, it zapped the cavity in my lower left molar, making me wince. "Ah-ah?" Swede said. "Ya sure now?"

Deciding he had either trips or two pairs, I pitched my cards into the muck.

"Missed your flush, huh? Too bad." He smoothed out his hand on the table: 10-10-10-2-2. As he pulled in the pot, he said, "Too bad for *Swede*."

Holy fucking shit. It could've cost me my bankroll if I'd hit the fifth diamond. Most guys with tens full would've mucked it face down, pretending they'd finessed you. I didn't get what he was up to. Just to prove how unreadable he was, which I already knew, he'd let me feel lucky and smart? "Nice hand, man," I said, almost laughing.

"Thanks, kid," he said. "I was just wonderin' somethin'. Ya know how jism clots up 'fore it swirls down the drain?"

So what, we were pals now? Even when we looped in the same foursome, all he'd ever say to me was, "You got the flag," or ask if I saw which bushes his player's wild tee-shot had stopped near. I finally said, "Yeah?"

"'Course ya do," he said, which completely broke everyone up. Trying not to blush, or blurt out that *he* was the jerker, I probably turned redder than Vogel had.

In the next half hour I won three decent pots, one by bluffing Tennessee, though I think Zrout bluffed me out of another one. Each new bankroll bottom line reminded me I could get a used Hawk or T-Bird for six or eight hundred. I'd even seen a '64 1/2 Mustang going for $1,125 in the *Trib*. It must've been in an accident or something, though as long as it went when I stepped on the gas, I'd be satisfied. Guys with cars and licenses made out like crazy, of course. Chicks like Laurie and Gina were tired of bike dates once they were freshmen or sophomores.

Swede's sorry ride was an orange-white '58 Sky Hawk, basically a Dreamsicle with rust, chrome, and wings, though if he heard you call it that you were toast. I had no idea what he'd paid, but the prices of Packards and Studes had been dropping since the plant closed a couple of years ago, which made it harder to get parts for them. His was no doubt even cheaper because of how ugly it was.

He and Tennessee had been pushing to make the antes a buck, and now all of a sudden they wanted that to be that. Standing up, Zrout said, "Forget it." He even yawned like he couldn't be bothered, instead of just saying, "I'm chicken. *Bwawk* buk-buk-buk . . ."

When no one else wanted the seat, we went on five-handed: me, Cziesla, Frick, Frack, and Vogel. My plan was to shuffle and deal slightly slower, and take longer to think before acting—to play as few hands as possible until another player or two got up the nerve to sit in.

Frick and/or Frack started raising every hand, as expected. It might've made it easier to trap them, but it cost you a dollar a hand while waiting for something tasty enough to bait your damn trap with. For the first three rounds I never found a pair above sixes, so there went three fins down the toilet in twenty-five minutes.

Finally someone in creased khaki chinos plunked down on my right: Charlie Rupp. "You guys mind if I play a few hands?" He's not only assistant CM but the club's only Chick Evans scholar, so what could we say? He didn't like Swede or Tennessee, but Stan wouldn't let him mess with their loops. To go with the hickey on his neck, he had on his red Ohio State Football golf shirt. Except for when he was kissing up to members, he called it "*the* Uh-hi-uh State University."

Cziesla said, "Seriously?"

"Of course not," said Charlie. "Mr. Evans himself, age seventy-five, would personally hand me my ass in a sling. I just need to do some reconnaissance."

My dad's told me six hundred times to apply for an Evans. When I remind him you can't until after your junior year, he tells me to ask Charlie how to "prequalify," whatever that's supposed to mean. He found out Evans applicants had to loop for two years at one club, maintain a B average, score 25 on the ACT, demonstrate financial need, and be of upstanding character, which in his mind means whitewall haircut, don't listen to the Stones, don't play poker. "I'll handle the financial need part, don't you worry." And since none of the Evans houses are at Catholic colleges, I guess that means, *ipso facto*, he's copacetic with me taking a pass on St. Stanislaus. Gramma freaked out, but not him, though he'd completely lose his shit if he knew I was here playing poker. And since Evans types try to make four loops a weekend, I couldn't serve Mass anymore. Maybe I could even get a subscription to *Playboy*, like Charlie had—just for the articles, of course.

After watching a few hands, he said, "Y'all hear about this other game?"

Swede grimaced, like *"Y'all"*? "What other game," he said, making it plain he didn't much cotton to college boys but was always on the lookout for action.

Charlie sat up straighter, all peppy and preppy. "At the Burmeisters'?"

Swede and Tennessee shook their heads. Though

nobody cared, I didn't either.

"Couple weeks ago, Bill and Nance Burmeister hosted this friendly little game at their house—the Casses, my parents, maybe one other couple. They've been playing awhile, Big Bill is shuffling, accidentally drops a card on the rug. When he leans under the table to pick it up, he can't help noticing Nora Cass, in one of her signature minis, has her legs spread, and more than a little. Turns out sweet little Nora ain't wearing no panties. Next hand, Bill makes sure to drop another card. Down he goes again, just to double-check. Sure enough, the bodacious Mrs. Cass is conveying, shall we say, *joie de beavre*."

Tennessee had stopped dealing, since nobody cared about draw anymore. Nora Cass was the consensus best-looking member of the club. Her only serious competition would be Janie Herron. Stan always gave them to crew-cut A-jocks like Sweeney, but Mrs. Cass and Mrs. Herron were my favorites to loop in the same foursome with. Mrs. Cass's toned legs reminded me of Laurie's or Marybeth's or Miss Moore's. Mrs. Cass's were even better in golf skirts, with the little white pompoms on the backs of her socks. Plus, she was easy to loop for: driver, 3-wood, 9-iron, putter. She also hit driver on the par 3's, with an extra 3-wood or two to reach the par 5's. Always in the fairway, hardly any traps to rake or divots to replace. No one ever said she flirted with her caddies, but a risqué story involving any member's wife would've been enough to slow down the action.

Mrs. Cass without panties? You could almost hear the boners knocking up into the table.

"But I mean," Vogel said, "how're *you* supposed to know what—"

"You deaf?" Cziesla said. "His parents were at the damn game."

"*Thank* you," said Charlie. We all knew his parents weren't members, either because they didn't golf much or couldn't afford the dues, though how was their son supposed to demonstrate financial need *and* afford a new Mustang? But they did play Hinsdale as guests a few Sundays a year. Of the Burmeisters.

"Anyway," said Charlie, "few hands later, Bill grabs the empties and heads to the kitchen to freshen folks' drinks, and who if it isn't the lovely Nora tagging alongside him. 'So, Billy,' she whispers, 'see anything you liked under there?' Now Bill's pretty shocked, but he's certainly got no complaints. 'S'matter a fact, toots, Ah did.' Nora flips her silky locks and starts touching his arm. 'Gosh, Billy, I'm tickled to hear that. I want you to know, it's all yours.' 'All mahn?' 'Every last little bit of it,' she coos. Then all of a sudden her voice gets more businesslike. 'But it's going to cost you, of course. A thousand dollars.'"

"Get the fuck outta here," said Vogel. Swede said, "One large for some tang?" while Cziesla and I yelled at Vogel to shut up and let Charlie finish. It wasn't just the subject, either. He was doing a really good job mimicking sweet Nora Cass going back and forth with

Burmeister's sly Texas drawl.

"My hand to God," he said. "I heard my dad telling my mom about it."

Swede looked annoyed. "So what's Burmeister say?"

"Big Bill thinks it over for maybe a second, says, 'Got yourself a deal, sugar. Just say where and when.' Nora says, 'Well, as you know, Tim's working Friday afternoons this summer, but *you're not*, so—' 'Ah'll be by at two, honeysuckle.'"

Charlie paused, basking like a tomcat in our horny attention. "Friday, two sharp, Burmeister knocks on the Casses' front door. Nora answers in saucy black lingerie, same kind Janet Leigh wore in *Psycho*. Migh-ty might-y fine, as we all can imagine. When he hands her the money she folds both McKinleys into one of the C-cups then leads him upstairs by his tie to the bedroom where, shall we say, their transaction is completed as promised. It's nasty, it's filthy, it's straight freakalicious. When it's over, completely wiped out, they share the *de rigueur* cigarette before Bill gets back in his clothes, hustles downstairs, and drives home." Charlie waited again. Except for the drips off the gutters, dead silence. "Tim Cass gets home around six. Finds Nora in the kitchen, plants a perfunctory kiss. 'Hi! How was work?' 'Oh, fine,' he says. 'Bill Burmeister happen to swing by today?'"

"Aw Jeez!" hooted Cziesla.

"Jeez is right," Charlie said. "Because Nora's like, *whoa!* After hemming and hawing, she says, 'Why, yes, dear, Bill dropped by for minute, but—' 'Did he give you a thousand bucks?' Nora's shitting an absolute brick now. 'Well, yes, dear, he *did.*' To which Tim replies, 'Good,' with a satisfied look on his face. 'Good?' 'Yeah, it's all good. He came by my office and borrowed it from me. Said he needed to pick up a few cases of Bordeaux—wine broker won't take a check? Anyway, he promised he'd stop by this afternoon and pay me back.'"

Charlie stopped talking, but it took me a moment to realize the story was over. The first clue was Tennessee baying like a demented coonhound. He eventually managed to wheeze, "Now *zat,* is a bluff, 'n' a half!"

"You fuckin' A," said Swede. "But it's not like—this actually happened?"

Palms up, Charlie shrugged like, *It happened.*

As Tennessee dealt the rest of the hand and guys fired questions at Charlie, it dawned on me that he might've overheard his parents talking about something Burmeister told his dad, but how could any of the Rupps know what happened in the Casses' kitchen? Not unless one of the Casses had told Charlie's dad . . . I was happy to find nines with an ace, but after Vogel opened for $3.50, I folded. Plus didn't Mrs. Cass have a kid? And it wasn't like she needed the money. Meanwhile Swede started laughing with or at Charlie in a way I couldn't interpret.

It's impossible to keep a stone face with your bladder howling like a banshee, so I needed to pee pretty soon. As soon as I got up, so did Charlie. When I knocked my bills together, Tennessee said, "Now hold on a sec, kid.

Ain't splittin' now, are ya?"

"Of course not. I just gotta piss."

"What you just gotta *do,*" said Swede, "is leave your wad right on the table."

"All of it?"

"Yep. Ever cent," said Tennessee. "Less you wanna buy y'seff a sody-pop."

I was hoping Charlie would either stay there and guard it or say it was okay to bring it with me, but he was already back in the office. "No one's rippin' nobody off here," said Swede, almost like his feelings were hurt.

"No one's saying anyone is." My eyeballs felt stingy, but I realized they were right. According to Hoyle, table stakes also means you can't take money off it: you have to give opponents the chance to win back what they lost. I'd only be ten feet away, but I still didn't want to leave it all out there, exposed. As of last week, most of it had been in the First Bank of Lisle, insured by the FDIC.

"Yer buddy-boys'll guard-dog it for ya," said Tennessee, nice and friendly, as if Vogel and Zrout as a tag team could stop him from snatching a twenty.

I counted it, laid it back down. "Hundred sixty-two, plus this," I said, setting a stack of quarters on top of the bills, like castling my rook with no king.

"Don't forget to wash them hands either," said Swede.

It felt good to walk a few steps. "Yeah yeah," I said, fighting the urge to look back as I turned the corner into the john.

Even when the green stall was empty—as it was

now, thank God—it still reeked of beer farts and piss. Above the urinal were the usual names and numbers to call for a BJ. I didn't even wonder anymore who might answer if you dialed one, or what I would say. As I zipped up, I spotted something new slanting down above eye-level, apparently written by a lanky southpaw with jittery penmanship.

> He who writes on shithouse walls
> rolls his shit in little balls.
> He who reads these words of wit
> eats those little balls of shit.

I stupidly looked away, in case the author burst in and caught me. As if. Yet I couldn't help thinking about getting tricked into eating one—a solid shit Milk Dud, say, mixed in with the regulars by some royal asshole at the Milk Dud factory, a suspiciously chewy one oozing past my molars and taste buds, halfway down my throat before I realize what's happening. Gah!

By one o'clock it was obvious nobody would be teeing off anytime soon, and most of the caddies had left. The problem was, it was costing me buck after buck to keep mucking all the toilet paper people kept dealing me, or I dealt to myself. Jack-4-7-9-3, 7-9-2-3-2. Four to a jack-high flush. Nines at the top of a straight draw, after Vogel raised Swede. I did make eights full once, but nobody called when I bet.

I was down to $125.35 when I squeezed out a

king-7-7-king . . . 9. Deciding to go for a checkraise, I passed. I wasn't even worried when Cziesla and Tennessee passed, since I knew Swede would go, "Three-fitty all day." Presto. After Vogel mucked, I pretended to think for a while, but without overdoing it. Plucking two fins from my stack, I laid them across the salad of quarters and singles. "Ten straight," I said, hoping my voice wouldn't crack. It did not.

Swede had already folded to two of my pre-draw reraises that day, a new record, but this time he looked positively tickled to call. That he used seven singles to do it I read as *not thrilled but let's gamble*. We both drew one card, which I reckoned made him a 5-to-1 dog to hit either a flush or a straight. Stackwise, he clearly had me covered, but I still said, "How much are you playing?"

He hated people asking him questions, so it surprised me when he didn't singe my eardrums with an ornery comeback. All he did was fan out his bills, making sure the twenties were at one end, then the sawbucks, the fins, and the singles. He didn't look nervous, but his lips tapped together as he toted it up. "One senny-seven. How much more *you* playin'?" He sounded both hostile and curious.

"One nineteen," I said right away, "plus this," pointing to my six bucks in change. I felt his blue stare on my eyelids as I squeezed out my cards extra slow, trying not to give away how much or little I liked them: 7 . . . 7 . . . king . . . The next one had a black horizontal serif at the bottom, but not at the top: an ace instead of a king. With kings up, ace kicker, I patted the table to check.

"Eighty," he said, slapping four twenties on top of the smaller bills.

"Gulp," said Tennessee.

"Yeah," I said, swallowing. "Like you got any business talking to me now."

"Any business *talkin'* to you?"

"Yeah, what gives with you, man?" I said, still not meeting his eye.

"What *gives* with me?" He was about to say something else, fighting words probably, when I saw Swede shoot him a look. The twelve guys still left in the room all shut up. "No, no, you're right," said Tennessee, leaning back while yanking a zipper across his thin lips. "Play your hand."

My heart was pounding so hard, there was no way my face wasn't giving off tells: that I hadn't filled up. If my fingers weren't pressing my cards to the table, they would've been shaking like madmen. So I kept them right there while trying to calm down and think straight. Way more often than not, Swede would bet everything here, so why "only" eighty? Because he wanted me to call? Or because he wanted me to think that he wanted me to? If I did call and won, I'd be almost halfway to a car. If I folded, I'd have enough to keep playing in huge games like this one. (Good idea? Maybe not.) If I called and lost, I'd only have forty-something, plus the $15.00 I'd left in the bank.

Creasing four twenties lengthwise, I scraped the eight edges up the front of my neck, round my chin, against the grain of my seventeen whiskers. Again, this time glancing from the pot to Swede's better-not-fuck-with-me face. And again.

"What he meant to say," he said, "was play your hand sometime this week."

"Okay, then I call," I said, tossing the twenties in. Fuck it.

Time speeded up as we showed down our hands, or my vision got blurry and jerky. I felt a knee in the small of my back as guys crowded closer. Groans, curses, whistles, and I think Swede said, "Huh." It must've been fear or adrenalin that kept me from seeing right away that we both had kings and sevens. "Holy majoly," said Vogel. Tennessee shook his head. "Looks like our man here got jacked up on his own whatyacallit." I'd been playing poker since I was a kid, but I seemed to be the last guy in the shack to realize my ace outkicked Swede's jack.

"Oh, wow," I said. "Jesus." Duh Vinci. As I pulled the pot toward me, some quarters spilled into my lap. I left them there, even when a couple of them bounced on the floor. I started grabbing the green and gray paper, starting with the twenties on top. Charlie, who was standing behind me, picked up the quarters and gave them to me. "His petard," he said, punching my shoulder. "Nice call, kid."

My lungs felt too fluttery to talk, even breathe with.

I was supposed to ask him how to prequalify, but obviously not right this minute. I wanted to play draw forever, blow off high school *and* college, just travel around like the Mavericks. I also was tempted to invent some excuse to stand up and lock in my profits. I wanted the sun to come out and Stan to assign me a loop, so I'd *have* to get up.

"Though with him attacking with most of his busts," Charlie was saying, "I can't see what you were thinking about." Swede meanwhile was barking up Tennessee's nostrils, something about "running your hillbilly mouth."

When Tennessee told him, "Let's go then," my money jumped up off the table. I hadn't finished stacking it yet. There it was, coins and bills floating in front of me, drifting toward my face in slow enough motion that I could pick out each president's face and weird collar before he whooshed past me. Out of focus, miles in the background, Tennessee and Swede were throwing haymakers—bombs—at each other. I tried to snatch bills from the air and got knocked off the bench. Breaking my fall with one hand, I rolled sideways into Cziesla and onto the floor. Everyone was whooping it up, grabbing money, yelling for the fighters to nail one another or stop. I wanted to see the fight too, but I needed to snatch back as many twenties as possible ASAP, since most of them had to be mine. Matchsticks and cinders biting into my kneecaps, one palm stuck to the crumbling brown tiles, I scanned for big bills. Forget the damn quarters and singles.

When I finally peeked back up, Sweeney and Zrout were helping Charlie and Stan pull them apart. Tennessee looked glad it was over. Not Swede. You could tell he was hurting, and not just because his face was maroon. Gulping huge breaths, he sounded like he meant it when he threatened, over and over and over, to kill Tennessee's inbred ass. Tennessee gasped and cackled. "Tell us 'bout it, Jerker," he said, with the Y. Which was roughly when Swede started puking.

"Hey!" I yelled from my knees when I saw a guy who hadn't been playing pick up a twenty. "That's mine and you know it!" He was a junior or senior and could've taken me easy, but I still would've fought him for it. One second he was like, *No way am I giving this back, twerp,* and the next he was crumpling it into a ball and firing it at my crotch. I bobbled it for a second, but caught it. He must've decided Stan or Charlie might've seen him. Turned out to be a sawbuck, but still.

After Stan and Charlie helped Swede to the john, Vogel helped me pick up the few last dimes and nickels on my side of the table. Avoiding the puke, which stank of rotten eggs and ammonia, Tennessee grabbed what was left of his and Swede's money from the floor by the window. "Git down here and help me!" he barked at some B-jocks. "Cough up what you stoled!"

A lot of my wad had landed pretty much on top of me. I didn't count it right then because I didn't want Tennessee eyeing it, but I wound up with $154.80, three bucks less than I came with, roughly sixty less than I should've had.

Outside, Vogel told me Swede had started it by elbowing Tennessee in the ribs. Swede got in solid shots before Tennessee kneed him in the balls at least twice. He went down and curled up, so he couldn't fight back as Tennessee pounded and choked him. Swede had him by a good thirty pounds, but Tennessee was just meaner. The tale of the tape doesn't always tell the whole story.

Swede didn't show the next day, but on Friday—get this—Stan put him and Tennessee out in a foursome together to force them to make nice, welts and black eyes and all. Yet everyone said that they did. I was still on the course when their foursome got finished. When mine straggled in around five, Charlie told me, "Things with those cats are perfectly groovy," though he didn't know how or if Tennessee had divvied up their money. The hitch was that Stan had decreed we all had to give poker a rest for a month. After that, Charlie said, Stan would see.

Vogel and his mom were waiting for me in their woody Merc wagon when Charlie took me aside by the steps going into the shack. For the third or fourth time, he told me there was no way they'd faked the fight just to get my nine twenties flying around. "But you're still nuts to play in that game." When I reminded him I'd been up ninety bucks when the fight started, he said, "Even so. No way in hell are you beating those guys in the long run."

"But didn't you say if they're whaling on each other they can't be ripping off B-jocks?"

"They'll figure *some*thing out, Vince." He put his hand on my shoulder but kept his arm straight. "That your kicker was an ace wasn't lucky? Just sayin' . . ."

When Mrs. Vogel tapped the horn, I waved and pointed to Charlie, her son's and my boss, a guy I could hardly turn my back on. "Maybe they're just better players than you," he was saying. "Not that you don't have a knack."

"Maybe they're not. You make a tough call and you're right, it's not luck."

He smiled and shook his head like, *What am I supposed to do with this guy?* "Rest assured that Miss Lucy won't always have her tongue in your ear."

"I know," I said, just to say it. The truth was, like old Herbert O., I believed in the immutable law of averages, that good players make their own luck.

"When Roscoe gets back, that's *tres hombres* you don't wanna mess with."

"I know," I said. "But hey. Do you know if Roscoe's lefty or righty?"

"If he's lefty or *righty?*"

"I was wondering because, I mean—"

"As in, is he sinister?"

I shook my head no. It was hot. I was hungry and thirsty.

"We shouldn't even let those types loop here. Either

way, you've got way better things to do at this club, down the road." He shook me a little. "Nome sayin'?"

"No no, I do," I said. "You're right. Stupid question."

It was obviously a mistake to argue with the assistant CM, the guy who could promote me to A by the end of the summer and walk me through the Evans application next year. That was my dad talking, though. Yardley and Vogel and our friends from St. Joan, maybe even Grampa Tom and Mr. Colarco, not to mention Uncle Thomas for sure, would be proud of me for playing in the hairiest game around, not to mention it being the only chance I had of affording my own wheels by the time I turned sixteen.

I looked past Charlie's car at all the members' Caddies and Lincolns, mostly in the shade of the trees now. I spotted two other Mustangs, plus Burmeister's Nassau blue Stingray over by the valet. "Speaking of tongues in guys' ears," I said, "did Burmeister screw Mrs. Cass?"

Mrs. Vogel honked twice. Letting go of my shoulder, Charlie tapped it three times with his fist. "You mean," he said, pulling back the screen door, "did Ah bluff Timmy Cass into paying hisself a grand to let me drill his own wahf?"

"Well—yeah."

He let the door creak shut between us. "Well, yeah, son, Ah did."

Picasso

I figured her face was the reason they called her that. One eye was green, the other gray-blue. I hadn't been close enough yet to get a good look, but the left one seemed wider sometimes, higher up, and from certain angles they seemed too close together. Other times, too far apart. Her nose wasn't perfectly centered, which made her cheekbones looked tilted. As in a Picasso, I guessed.

The first time I got a decent look at her she was kneeling in front of some lockers, the beige ones near the end of the second-floor hallway. She was crucified in the standard skirt-check posture: chin up, back straight, arms parallel to the floor. She must be double-jointed because with her palms facing down her fingers curved upward as she held them together. So steady. One of the nuns crouched beside her, black habit pooling on the tiles. Head cocked sideways, she was zeroing in on Picasso's plaid skirt.

"Oh my goodness, young lady."

Picasso said nothing. She shifted her weight from one knee to the other, but her face didn't show any pain.

The nun, clucking and tsking, had her back to me, with her veil draped over her shoulder. I couldn't tell which one it was. "Oh my," she said, straightening up. "This is quite serious."

No response from Picasso. Her maroon blazer, buttoned once below her ribs, was pulled taut across her. I swallowed.

"Let me see here," the nun said, circling with little jab steps, like a crow getting ready to peck out the eyes of a live baby rabbit. It was Sr. Mary Walter, who taught Latin IV. She was also the Associate Dean of Discipline. "This is *quite* serious," she said, twirling the ends of her cincture. "Oh my my my my . . ."

I didn't turn around, but I sensed a few gawkers had stopped. Other gawkers, I guess. "Nothin's more lewd than the mind of a prude," one girl whispered. My ears and cheeks started to burn.

"At least four inches there," Walter said. "Maybe five. Five whole inches, young lady, from that hem to the floor."

The rule was that uniforms had to cover girls' knees. Some of the fast ones rolled their skirts at the waist, to show off the backs of their knees, but they had to unroll them when the nuns or priests went on the warpath. That's how it worked at St. Joan, but in high school they seemed to make a bigger deal about it, maybe because the girls were more voluptuous now.

"Five at *least* . . ."

Picasso continued to stare, barely moving, past me, past the gawkers, at nothing. She winced as she shifted her weight again, then shook her head and smiled to take it back. I noticed that her skirt wasn't rolled.

Walter meanwhile had brought out her pad of detentions. "Remain, young lady, just as you are," she cawed, noting the time on her watch.

I heard a guy clearing his throat, and a girl right behind me whispered, too loud, "It's Picasso." Another girl—Mary Mannion, I think—made wet chomping noises. People quietly hooted until Walter hissed, "Cease!"

The gawkers backed up and scattered. When the bell rang it scattered them faster. I had to go too, since my next class was on the first floor.

"You'll've had that hem lowered tomorrow," cawed Walter, "or indeed you will *not* bother coming."

Picasso glanced up at me for a second, then refocused on nothing. "I can't sew," she told Walter.

Walter tore off the pink slip and tried handing it to her, but Picasso kept her fingers locked together in the same curved position, like saluting *Sieg heil!* in two directions at once, though not like a Nazi—like Walter was the Nazi and Picasso was the beautiful Jewess. When Walter swung around to see who she'd looked at, I backed away toward the stairs. There was no one behind me, just the three of us left in the hallway, as Walter tried giving her the detention again.

No dice.

Dashing down the stairs, I heard Walter caw, "That's it, you. Get up! *Up*! Right now! To my *office*!"

Over the next several weeks I went out of my way—following her in the halls, keeping my ears open around seniors and juniors, even asking Ellen a couple of "innocent" questions—to find out what gave with this chick.

At first I'd assumed her last name was really Picasso. Though she didn't look Spanish, it was the only way people ever seemed to refer to her. So that's what I called her too, in my mind. Even later.

When I asked Ellen, "What's going on with this Picasso?" she told me her real name was Linda Krajacik. She'd started at St. Procopius in September, though Ellen didn't know from what school, or even what state, she had transferred. But she had Fr. Albin for chemistry and Tim White for English, which meant she was one of the smart ones. "Ain't she a bit old for you, sonny? Though I guess old Miss Moore's still got a few years on her . . ." Which was when I stopped asking her questions.

Picasso's earlobes were pierced, and she usually wore little gold circles. Her hair was a bronze, grainy color, with bangs past her eyebrows. You could tell that she didn't use hair spray. She didn't wear nylons or penny loafers, or a senior boy's ring. She did not go to pep rallies, sock hops, basketball games, or join any clubs. She did not get along. As far as I could tell, the only people she'd talk to were teachers, but only when she got called on, and sometimes not even then. I heard her name at least three times over the PA for after-school detention duty. She was one of the very few girls who made that list even once.

She lived in Western Springs and drove to school by herself in a red MG Midget. Kevin McTeague from my Latin class told me her Illinois license was suspended, so she was using one from the state she'd just moved from. Zrout said that was legal, but most people, including my dad, said it wasn't.

She never ate lunch. She just sat by herself in the glassed-in corner of the cafeteria, reading *The Brothers Karamazov*. Her father supposedly didn't live with her and her mother—either that or he'd died. She got stoned every morning, which was why her pupils were always dilated. She was anti the Vietnam War, even though her brother was over there fighting. Ellen said she'd heard he'd been killed.

A month after I saw Walter checking her skirt, there was graffiti on the wall of the second-floor john. Block letters, black magic marker: HONORABLE GOOK SAY PICASSO SLURP LONG HIPPIE SHLONG. I wanted to rub it off, or scribble something over it, but the john was too crowded. By the time I went back the next day the janitors had done the job for me. (Only the most harmless graffiti lasted more than an hour at Proco.) The glossy white finish of both of the tiles had been sanded, though if you knew what to look for you could still make out some of the words.

During study hall once I went to the shelf of the library where they kept all the art books, going alphabetically till I came to Picasso. The book with his paintings had maybe fifty reproductions, and they looked like the work of more than one guy. They weren't what I'd've called beautiful, but some of the faces did remind me of Linda's. I could see how the seniors and juniors came up with the name. "Straight off some freakin' Picasso, man." In the *Portrait of Maya with a Doll* the little girl's features were literally all over the place; you could see the front of her face and the side, both at once. *Les Demoiselles d'Avignon* made me nervous. In *Girl with a Mandolin*, my favorite, the girl was completely naked—or nude, as you were supposed to say when it was art. The problem was that on the breast that wasn't blocked by the mandolin, her nipple was shaped like a trapezoid, and the other breast was basically triangles. She only had one eye, and no mouth. But even here I could see the similarities with Linda. Cock-eyed, off-kilter, whatever. I got it.

It also reminded me of Brian Jones playing lead on his teardrop Vox Phantom Mark III, except for the nude part, and the fact that he wasn't a girl.

According to the dust jacket of *Life with Picasso,* the author, Françoise Gilot, was "the woman who was Picasso's mistress for ten years. . . . Here is the intimate, extraordinary biography of this century's greatest artist," the key words being *mistress* and *intimate.* But I also wanted to find out why Picasso did the bodies and faces that way. Cubist nudes.

In the first chapter Françoise meets Pablo at a restaurant in Paris. She's twenty-one and he's *sixty-two*, and he's already been married four times! What the fuck. But I still skimmed ahead for the good parts. She visits him in his studio, he shows her his paintings, he goes to a gallery to see some of *her* paintings. His own can't be shown in any gallery because the Nazis occupying the city say his work is "degenerate." Like a grampa with a college girl isn't?

On page 28, Françoise and Pablo are looking out a window at "a cubist pattern formed by the roofs and chimney pots of the Left Bank." The next thing she knows, he "moved his hands up and lightly cupped them over my breasts." Two sentences later he takes his hands *off* them, "not suddenly, but carefully, as though my breasts were two peaches whose form and color had attracted him; he had picked them up, satisfied himself that they were ripe but then realized that it wasn't yet time for lunch."

It surprised me that Proco's library stocked stuff like this as I riffled the next dozen pages, scanning with my finger for lunchtime. Françoise rides her bike through the rain to his studio. When he sees that her hair's wet, he takes her to the bathroom and dries it himself, even though he's got like five servants. But then his male secretary, Jaime Sabartés, starts hassling them, so nothing really happens for a while. And I was like, fire that secretary! Hire a woman, like a normal businessman, for God's sake! Taste the peaches!

Finally, on page 47: "Picasso linked his arm through mine and guided me into the bedroom. In the middle of the room he stopped and turned to me. 'I told you I wanted to get an idea about something,' he said. 'What I really meant was that I wanted to see if the idea I already have is right.' I asked him what the idea was. 'I want to see if your body corresponds to the mental image I have of it. Also, I want to see how it relates to your head.' I stood there and he undressed me." If the line works that perfectly, you'd have to be crazy not to become a painter, though all he really does now is study her body and say, "You know, it's incredible the degree to which I prefigured your form." Then they lie on the bed and . . . keep talking!

I've been prefiguring your form for five years now, Dory, and I just wanna see if your breasts correspond to . . .

Yeah, right.

I skimmed two more chapters for sex scenes, but Françoise has clammed up on the subject. She also never says why Picasso did faces that way, or what it was like screwing a guy with white chest hair, presumably pubic hair too.

The middle of the book had glossy pages with black-and-white photos: Françoise and Pablo, their kids Claude and Paloma, Pablo's other wives, other kids, other mistresses. There was a funny one of Pablo marching behind Françoise on a beach, shielding her from the sun with an umbrella. Even a decent bikini shot of her, though her arm is blocking one of her breasts. Great legs, though, and whatnot.

It floored me that Pablo was able to land all these babes. You could see how twenty-two-year-old English rockers would be making them hand over fist, but an old, short, gray, bald guy? Yet here was the evidence right in this book, not to mention in *Time, Life,* etc. European chicks must just have a weakness for rich, cockeyed painters, I guess.

After making sure no one was looking, I tore out the page with the bikini shot and slid it into my geometry book. That way I'd make sure to put in plenty of time studying that night, especially tangents and trapezoids.

Second week of March, Saturday night, ten o'clock or a few minutes after. I was hitchhiking on Ogden, on my way home from the poker game at Keough's house in Naperville. His parents came home early and kicked us out, which was just as well because I was up almost twenty-four bucks. But it was still pretty cold, with not many cars on the road, and the ones that were weren't stopping. Swain Chevy's lights had just switched themselves off when a little red sports car pulled over.

Picasso.

She looked me over through her half-rolled-down window, making sure I wasn't Richard Speck or anything. "The Last Time" was playing. I opened my pea coat and grinned like a clod so she'd realize I wasn't a killer.

"Jump in," she said. "Let's go."

I climbed into the little bucket seat, slammed the door. The Stones weren't on the radio—it was a fancy black tape deck. "Thanks for stopping," I said.

She shifted into first, popped the clutch, and roared off. She was wearing a fringed buckskin jacket over an inside out T-shirt. "The Last Time" ended while we were stopped at a light, and "Good Times" came on. When the light changed I watched her shift gears, work the clutch. Her bell-bottoms flapped back and forth.

I realized I should probably stop gaping at her. "There's cops along here . . ."

"Are there, or is there?" She was already doing fifty-five, sixty.

I nodded and shrugged. "Sometimes, I guess." How would *I* know? I had my learner's permit, but I couldn't take the tests for my license for another six days.

"You go to Proco, correct?"

I nodded. She stared ahead at the road, dimming her brights for an oncoming car, shifting twice. "Vincent Killeen, right?" she said. "Ellen's brother."

"Vince."

"You're a sophomore," she said.

I admitted it.

"So you're what? Like sixteen?"

"Not till the twenty-second," I said.

She put her hand up on my biceps. "Kinda young for your age, then," she said.

"I guess," I said. "For a sophomore."

She reached down between the seats and pulled up a thin, twisted cigarette. I knew right away what it was.

She let out the clutch and accelerated, snapping my head back. "So, Vince. Do a reefer with me?"

"I really could use one," I said.

She placed it between her pale, pouty lips, shifted from second to third, pulled out a box of matches. "Shift for me, will ya?"

Fourth gear, I knew, was straight behind third. I'd never driven a manual, but the Midget's gear pattern was engraved on the knob of the shifter.

She took a wooden match from the box. "We ready?"

"Yeah," I said, desperate to sound nonchalant. "Go ahead."

She pushed in the clutch and I jerked the stick back. The first couple inches it came fairly smooth, but it caught near the middle and groaned. The struck match illuminated her weird, pretty face. "Pull," she said, lighting the joint.

I finally got the stick free by shaking it sideways, forcing it back toward me. Picasso inhaled. The little engine roared as she let out the clutch and we quickly lost all our momentum.

I'd put the damn thing into second.

"Missed it," she said, holding her breath. She waved out the match, shook her head.

"I thought . . ."

Our knuckles brushed together as she passed me

the joint. "Me too," she said. She pushed in the clutch, eased the stick toward my thigh, shoved it back up into third. "Smoke it," she said.

Flimsy and weightless, it flared and popped as I took my first puff. I hacked and gagged, doing my best not to cough. "The Under Assistant West Coast Promotion Man" came on as I carefully transferred the wet, twisted end to her thumb. She took three tiny drags, inhaled through her nose, took three more. "Where you headed?"

"Home," I said, exhaling. My left eye was watering. "Oakview."

"That's in Lisle, right?"

I looked out the window, at the glass of the window itself, then back at Picasso. "Yeah, Lisle." She looked at me funny while trying to pass me the reefer. I took it. This time I concentrated on taking a drag without coughing.

"You're home then."

I looked out again and saw we were over by Dooley's Garage. Oakview was a mile or so south of the next light, at Main.

She exhaled a plume of smoke. "But hey. Wanna go for a driiiive?"

I needed to cough, but I caught it by clearing my throat. "Absolutely." As she had been doing, I answered while holding my breath.

"Where to?"

I passed her the reefer, exhaled. "You mean, to

where?"

"Ah-hah. Is this why they call you Duh Vinci?"

My curfew was midnight. My parents were in Cleveland for some "retreat meeting" now that my dad was the sales manager, but Gramma would certainly be waiting up for me, praying and biting her nails. "Anywhere, really," I said.

Picasso blew her bangs from her eyes. "Don't matter, you're saying?"

I nodded and said, "I mean, no." I'd never felt stupider. With Margie and Laurie, or Dory and Gina, conversations went much much more smoothly.

She hung a left at Ogden and Main, working her way through the gears as we headed north toward the tollway.

"You're name's Linda, right?" I hardly could call her Picasso.

She nodded. When "That's How Strong My Love Is" started, she touched a lever on the deck, making the tape whine and whir till "Satisfaction" came on. We were on the eastbound ramp now, and she cranked up the volume. By the time she'd worked through the gears again the Midget's speedometer said just under ninety.

Only our knuckles would touch as we passed one another the joint. Pebbles and cracks in asphalt vibrated up through my scrotum. She danced in her seat while we listened to "Satisfaction" again, which you never could do with a radio.

"Made loud to be played loud," I said.

She nodded, though she might not've heard me. It was too loud to talk, but I wanted to tell her that Keith used a fuzzbox and special tuning to make his guitar sound that nasty—his red Gibson SG, solid body, with double humbuckers and devil horns. Mick was trying to make some girl, and it just wasn't happening, though he'd obviously made plenty of others. What I wouldn't go into was that whatever's the opposite of becoming a priest, except for the smoking part, that's what the song was about. I'd tell her they'd recorded it right in Chicago, in one of those studios on the South Side where Negroes played jazz and the blues.

When we got near the toll booths at Oak Brook she slowed down and flicked what was left of the reefer outside. You called that a roach. You could go to jail for ten years if they found one on your person, or even in a car you were in. "We're cool now," she said.

I squinted and swallowed as we drove through the plaza. Horizontal grooves in the concrete made the tires clatter and vibrate through my balls to my throat. It felt good. Picasso pulled down her visor and headed for the exact-change booths on the left. "Think they got enough *lights* on?" As she arched her back to dig into her pocket, I could see the contours of her breasts, maybe even a nipple pushing up through the T-shirt. A thimble, more like. Not a trapezoid.

"Got a nickel?" she said.

I should've had it ready for her! I quickly pulled some change from my pocket. We'd been playing for nickels, dimes, and quarters at Keough's, so there was a ton of it. Though I only had twelve paper dollars on me, I felt pretty proud of myself.

She opened her hand next to mine. "*Merci beaucoup, Monsieur Killeen.*"

I picked out a nickel and stared at it, trying to think how to say *You're welcome* in French. She took it, jangling it together with other coins in her hand. Turning away from me, she reached out the window, aimed, made a squeaky little sigh, and said, "Yesss!" As soon as the gate swung up, she began to accelerate. "I owe you a nickel," she said.

We cruised along into the blackness, though the moon was up over Chicago. With its craters and mountains and valleys it looked like a black-and-white version of Earth. Its light somehow made the new concrete tollway seem to be flowing back *toward* us . . .

Picasso touched my left knee and pointed to the glove box. "Cigarettes," she said. "Gotta have one."

I felt around among the maps and sunglasses and came up with a hardpack of Marlboros. I pulled out two, lit them, handed one over. I wanted to ask whether she'd had Mr. Dennerlein last year for geometry but remembered that this was her first year at Proco. I wanted to ask where her father and brother were. To tell her that if she didn't want me to call her Picasso, or even think of her as Picasso, I wouldn't.

"How come I dig you so much?" she said. "'Cause we're stoned?"

"Maybe," I said. Grass made you dig people more? "I don't know."

"Saint Pro-co-pi-us, man. D'you know those loony Benedictines are heirs of the Druids?"

I couldn't tell whether she was serious. "They are?"

"Absofuckingtootly. St. Bernard and the Druids're who it all *started* with."

"Huh. Not with Benedict and Scholastica?"

She coughed, shook her head. "Three drops of milk from the breast of a black Celtic virgin, or something like that."

I shook my head, trying to picture that.

"Those fucking nuns worship werewolves," she said, grabbing my forearm and squeezing, which gave me a nuclear doozer. She rubbed her hands back and forth a few times, patted my arm, put both hands back on the wheel. "I had to drop my old lady off at O'Hare. It's my birthday, ya know."

"Happy birthday," I said. "If I'd known I'd've gotten you something."

"Hey, I'm sure you would've. Just, only, no spanking, okay? All I ask."

"If you say so."

"Think I'm jukin' you, don't ya?"

"What makes you say that?"

She pulled something from her pocket and handed it over. Her driver's license. "See?" In the picture her hair was darker and wavier. I only was sure it was her from the lopsided tilt of her face. Her birth date was

March 16, 1949. "That's today, offisuh."

"You're seventeen?"

She held her palm open like, *Hey, do the math.*

"Just thought you were sixteen."

"I was, Vince. Just was." She seemed to be getting older—older than I was, at least—by the minute. "Private party at my house," she said. "Wanna come?"

"Nous y voici," she said, leading me into the living room, which was as big and fancy as you'd guess from the size of the house. Her moccasins had no heels, so with my black mod boots on I was taller. She shrugged off the buckskin jacket, tossed it on a chair, disappeared round a corner. "Give me *one* minute," she called.

The living room had overstuffed chairs, a leather couch, fancy globe, fancy stereo console, big speakers, a couple of paintings of boats in a harbor definitely not by Picasso. *Lifes* and *National Geographics* covered most of the coffee table. The cover of one *Life* showed a couple of soldiers in a ditch with their faces wrapped in bandages. I couldn't tell if they were Marines. I'd probably join up when I graduated, one way or the other, though if I got a deferment I wouldn't be going till I finished college, if the war wasn't over by then.

I thought about calling Gramma and telling her I'd sleep over at the Keoughs', like that had been the plan all along, but she might ask to talk to Mr. or Mrs. She always used to give me the benefit of the doubt on things, but she hadn't really been my biggest fan since

I stopped serving, especially since I "reneged" on my "commitment" to enter the seminary. There was maybe a five percent chance she'd be asleep by the time Picasso drove me home, or I hitched. My curfew was midnight, and it was already 10:42. She'd let me slide for fifteen or twenty minutes, but if I wasn't home by midnight she'd probably call the Naperville cops, my parents in Cleveland, or both. But even if I'd get grounded for a decade when my parents got home, what was I supposed to say when Picasso invited me over? I'd get home when I got home, and whatever would happen would happen.

When she came back in she was barefoot, with a glass in each hand, balancing a huge blue ceramic ashtray on her forearms. "Cuervo and Coke," she said. "All we had." She put down the ashtray and handed me one of the glasses. "To me," she said, raising her own.

We clinked. "Happy birthday," I said.

We both took long sips. The tequila's peppery-oniony taste burned through the Coke and surprised me. I liked it. And I liked it when she went over to the console with her pocketless jeans cupping her butt. Dust crackled through the speakers before Marianne Faithfull's version of "As Tears Go By" started playing. As I took another long swig, I wanted to ask where her mother had flown to—pretty weird if it was Cleveland—or if she'd figured out yet why she dug me. Did she even have a brother? Where was her dad? I lit two more Marlboros and handed her one. The tequila was starting to hit me.

After only one puff she snuffed out her cigarette, moved the ashtray onto the floor, and slid over, pressing her knees against mine. She fingered my chin and said, "Kiss."

She opened her mouth when I kissed her, turned her head sideways, pushed her tongue against mine. It tasted like vaguely sweet cigarettes, and I kissed her as hard as I could. When she pulled back her head and sat up, I thought I had blown it somehow, but she smiled, put her glass on the table. I snuffed out my cigarette.

This time when we kissed she ran her fingers through my hair and grabbed my right elbow, adjusting my arm so my hand ended up on her hip. I kept my eyes closed and tried to enjoy what was happening. She kissed me on the nose and stood up, unzipped her jeans, shimmied out of them. My erection was caught against the back of my zipper, and I needed to move it. I reached for my drink.

"Happy birthday," I said.

"Sip, *s'il vous plaît.*"

She took one from my glass and knelt down. "I'm digging you kind of a lot, Vince Killeen."

I looked at her knees, at her bangs, trying to think what to say. She put my glass on the table. I decided she was doing all this because I hadn't asked *why.*

"Help me," she said, standing up. She started unbuttoning my shirt, then stepped back and switched off the lamp. My eyes weren't used to the dark, but I watched her as hard as I could as she crossed her arms and pulled the T-shirt up over her head. I was hoping she'd smile, or something like that, but she didn't. She looked like she was settling some serious business, though all she had on were dark panties. In the light from the hallway her breasts looked much more 3D, and at the same time more delicate, than I'd expected, though it's hard to say *what* I expected.

"Y-you," I said, stuttering, "I . . ." I tossed my shirt onto the couch. My erection was painful as I looked at her thighs, at her navel. I remembered the first time I saw her, kneeling like that on the floor. I remembered Angie and Misty kneeling like that, back at St. Joan.

"I?" said Picasso. I couldn't help shivering as she ran her cold fingers across my chest. "Now *you* have a very cool bod."

Still standing, barely touching, we started kissing again. Picasso's strange eyes stayed open, though they looked less crooked up close. A car screeched to a halt down the block and I waited for the sound of the impact. We kissed. Picasso had turned us around, tilting us sideways and back while keeping her tongue in my mouth, easing me down by my shoulder and hip, maneuvering us so that when we finally stopped turning and sinking her body was stretched out in front of me, her head on my left, and I was kneeling on the floor leaning over her. Our tongues kept stabbing, exploring. Our teeth clicked a couple of times. I didn't do it on purpose, but somehow my right thumb briefly brushed the lower left edge of her panties. When I moved it back down, the tiny hairs above her warm kneecap gave us both zaps of electricity. The skin on the inside was cool and smooth as Formica.

As it dawned on me that I was about to have sexual intercourse, I was like, What's the catch? A Catholic girl putting out, maybe ready to go all the way? Forty minutes after you meet her? And it's all her idea?

The most important thing was not to get overexcited, to act like I'd been around this block a few times. Maybe dozens. The main problem was, I still had my pants on, with no clue about how to get free long enough from the kissing to take off my boots, undo my belt, and unzip. The next thing I knew Picasso stopped kissing and was guiding my face toward her breasts. She also shifted her hips in a way that pushed the satiny crotch of her panties against my right hand.

The heated mound underneath wasn't quite what I'd expected. I tried massaging it with my palm, using the same motion and pressure as if she'd been hit by a foul tip, while concentrating on giving her nipples an equal amount of attention with my teeth, lips, and tongue. It wasn't that easy to coordinate these operations.

"Master Killeen," she said, coaxing my head toward her belly. I was licking the gossamer hairs below her navel before I figured out *oh my God* what she wanted. "Yeah, Vinci." No way! The best plan, I thought, was to keep moving down on my own, stopping only when I'd reached her right knee. This would give me more time to get my bearings, plan my next measures, and maybe unbuckle my belt.

The aroma surprised me as I nuzzled my way past her panties. It smelled like a cross between shrimp, warm sweat, and a freshly mown lawn. Before I could make my next move Picasso arched her back, hooked her thumbs in her panties, and pushed them down past her hips. There she was. Any more balking on my part would give away what I was thinking. I pulled the panties the rest of the way off her legs. Oh my God. She slid her foot down to the floor and nudged the inside of my knee, making it clear what she wanted.

I'd been able to gather, mostly from studying *Modern Man* and *Playboy*, that a woman's most sensitive spot was her clitoris. "Like this miniature dick," Swede had said, "so a course only faggots'll french it." Few things could be more degenerate. The "big deed," according to him, was killing somebody, but frenching a clit was right up there. Maybe because it was too close to brownnosing—a couple three inches at most, so how could your nose *not* get involved? Vogel and Reid and McTeague called it muff-diving, or "giving sluts head." Krawdick told us his brother Stan had clued him in on the gory details. "Like I wanna get blood or the clap on my face? All these crabs in your nose, burrowing through to your brain?" Officially it was called cunnilingus, from the Latin for cunt licking, though we were still waiting for it to show up on a vocab quiz. Nice girls were supposed to hate it because (1) they were so touchy about everything taking place in that vicinity, and (2) they could hardly confess it. Speaking *ex cathedra*, Pope Paul said sex was for procreation, period, and you couldn't make a kid with saliva. Even dirty songs didn't mention it, let alone explain how it worked. I'd had to look up in *Webster's Collegiate* the whereabouts and function of ovaries, vulvas, monses, perineums, vaginas, and labia.

Linda moaned and breathed in as soon as my tongue touched her labia. Pretty tangy—like liver, uncooked but still warm. They were already moist but did not smell or taste much like pee. More like liver with vinaigrette dressing, and who would eat something like that? Duh Vinci Killeen. As I searched for her clitoris, she kept groaning and grabbing my hair, basically directing the search party.

After two or three minutes of scoping things out, I'd started to wonder if Linda in fact *had* a clitoris, or if Webster's had somehow misled me. Even using both hands, I'd found nothing "erectile," though from the way she was writhing and the tone of her voice while repeating my name, you'd've thought I had already found it.

My jawbones and ears were suddenly clamped between her thighs, so all I could move was my tongue. It was like her whole body was trembling. And then, just as suddenly, she'd opened her legs and was pulling me up toward her face, which was not a good time for me to yell, "Fuck!" As I'd got off my knees a charley horse in my thigh jerked me sideways. I hopped around frantically between the couch and the coffee table, trying to put weight on that heel.

"You okay?"

"I just gotta . . . Jesus!"

When I'd finally done it, I collected myself and began to undo my belt and my jeans. Linda reached up and unzipped them. I pushed down the jeans and my jockeys and felt her hand on my cock. I hoped she would think it was big enough. I fought not to come as she turned her hand over, brushing along the bottom with the backs of her fingers. Then she grabbed it again. "Hurry," she said, letting go.

I knelt on the couch with my knees between hers. Her breathing seemed louder—suddenly *too* loud, in fact—till I realized that side of the record had ended. I heard myself breathe along with her.

"I'm on the pill, so don't worry," she told me, but all I wanted to know at this point was whose responsibility it was to get me inside her. "Don't *worry.*"

I felt myself getting softer, at least till I looked at her again.

"It's cool."

Waiting much longer or saying anything else would betray my virginity. I leaned forward, like doing a pushup, letting my chest graze her breasts. I pulled back my hips, aiming at the spot where the opening was, and pushed down as hard as I could. Jesus Christ! My cock glanced off bone and smooshed sideways, and the pain ground my molars together.

Linda was doing her best not to laugh. *"Grrrr,"* she said, nipping my shoulder. She slid her hand between us and grabbed what was left of my boner, licking the spot where she'd bit me. "Move back," she said, guiding me with one hand, adjusting my hip with the other. The next thing I knew I was in her and something slippery and hot was clenching and releasing itself on my cock. I'm doing it, I realized. *I've done it!* Her heels were dug into the small of my back, her fingernails scraping my ass, before I remembered I was supposed to be screwing her. I reared back and shoved myself deeper and immediately felt myself start to come.

"No—shit!" I whispered.

She rose up to meet me, jamming us up to the hilt, sliding back. And again. I shivered, felt like killing myself, and ejaculated.

The slurp as I tried to pull out was almost as humiliating, but her calves and heels held me in tight. I wanted to somehow persuade her that, with me, things like this usually went differently.

The telephone rang, so up-close and loud that I jumped. Picasso reached back and grabbed it before the second ring started. She seemed not to mind what I'd done.

What I hadn't.

"Hello?"

As my cock shrank down and cooled off, I was scared it was gonna fall out.

"Of course," she said, as a woman's voice vibrated through the receiver. "Yes. Fine."

I laid there and tried to relax, though I had to piss

rather fiercely. Linda had lowered her legs and was kneading my spine with her knuckles. There were many long pauses, while the woman did most of the talking. "I'll try to remember that, Mother. Those were *her* suitcases, though. Are you nuts?" She put her index finger over my lips and looked in my eyes like, *Didn't* we *just have fun?*

"Of course," she said, tickling the side of my ribs. I twisted and gasped, almost yelping. When I looked up, she beamed at me, cross-eyed and goofy. "I mean *no.* No, of *course* not."

I tried to imagine what Picassoesque features her mother might have. "You're kidding." She'd started to move underneath me, rotating her pelvis in regular ovals. Her heart thumped through my nipple, and I smelled her warm sweat. "I gotta go too," she said finally. "Got a jillion things still left to pack."

My penis had started to swell—to ache on the inside, sting on the outside. Even weirder, I didn't have to piss any more.

"Okay," she said. "Fine. Just don't *worry.* It's all written down on the pad." Her mother went on now for almost a minute as Picasso rocked back and forth, but sometimes, even better, diagonally. "I know that," she said. "And I will." She kissed the receiver. "You too, Mother. Bye." She hung up. "Now exactly where were we?" she said. Our crotch bones ground against each other as I shoved myself further inside her, trying to build up a rhythm. "Oh right," she said. "Riiiight . . ."

I could tell I wouldn't come quite as fast this time, maybe because I was so hard that it hurt. Yet the faster I screwed her, the farther her hips inched away from me, and the tangle of pants round my ankles made it impossible to move forward while staying in rhythm.

"Wait a sec," she whispered. "Slide down."

We shimmied ourselves back till my toes hit the arm. I dug in. She braced her hands above her head, giving both of us more leverage. More than anything now I wanted my buddies at school and the golf course to know what was happening. Ellen and Dory and Gina, Angie and Misty. (Not Laurie.) Maybe not tonight, but sooner or later. In detail. Not for me to announce it, or for Linda to tell anyone, but for people to somehow find out on their own. And for me then to still never mention it.

"Oh *yeah,*" Linda said, taking fast breaths through her mouth. "It's da *Kid.*"

I raised myself up on my hands and looked at her face. I knew people might disagree, but I thought she looked crazy and beautiful.

She pulled her legs back by her shoulders and let me scoop her up closer to my end of the couch, which worked even better. She seemed to focus on receiving me into herself as gingerly as she could. The way she sounded and looked really encouraged me, boosting my energy, and we continued like this for longer than I had expected. Mainly I got off on watching her face, her strange eyes. She wouldn't let me look away either.

In the light from the hall, the way she was wincing and clenching her teeth, damp hair slicked back off her forehead, she actually looked like a Picasso.

Romeoville

I didn't find out until the next morning that Mike Figueroa was dead. Vogel, at whose house we had played dealer's choice, called me up. I grabbed the receiver off the kitchen wall after eight or nine rings, because God only knew where everyone else in my family was. Vogel started practically yelling that three minutes after we'd left his house in the Meadows, Figueroa's Impala slid through a red or yellow light at the intersection of Maple and Rt. 53 and got caught flush in the driver's side by a piggyback semi headed north on 53. Or maybe the light had been green. "Anyway, dead on arrival," he said in a more normal voice. "Impala got totaled."

"Wait—what, you're serious?"

"As two dogs with heart attacks doing it."

"You're saying Figueroa is dead."

"No, Duh, I'm calling to wish you—that's what I'm trying to tell you. He's dead."

Which is when I remembered the dream I was

having when the phone woke me up: some guy was telling me Figueroa's car had been *totaled*, a word my friends and I had been throwing around, now that we all had our licenses. But I also probably dreamt it because I'd imagined something like this happening to him. I daydreamed it five or six thousand times in the last month and a half, since he took Laurie Langan to Homecoming. I'd always thought dances like that were sub-idiotic—and that dreams were supposed to be trickier. I never prayed for Figueroa to die in a vicious explosion of gas, glass, and metal. I never challenged him to a fight or a drag race, or did anything to cause the crash to happen, like signing up for mechanic school to learn how to diddle with his brakes. I just daydreamed about it and presto. Shivering there in the kitchen in my plaid flannel boxers, I almost burst out laughing. It had happened about nine hours before I dreamt it, but still.

"Remember?" said Vogel. "Started snowing 'round nine, when we first snuck out to smoke on the patio. It'd stopped by the time you guys left."

"But getting warmer, not colder . . ." I sneezed.

"My old man might get nailed just for letting him drive after curfew."

Though Vogel couldn't see me, I nodded. Looking around for a napkin or tissue, I found a note my dad had left on the counter: AT THE JEWEL. HOME BY 10. START YOUR HOMEWORK! It was 9:47.

"Anyway, look," Vogel said. "Gotta go. My mom's completely freaking. Dudes from the coroner's office are over here grilling my old man right now."

About the only thing unusual about the game Friday night was that we hadn't been drinking, and that, I assumed, was what would get his old man off the hook. During most of our games, we hammered back whatever beer, wine, or hard stuff we'd managed to boost from our parents or have bought for us by college guys with IDs. Mr. Vogel had said we'd not only never set foot in his house again if we disturbed so much as a mote of dust on his wine racks, he'd call the cops on us if he even suspected we'd been drinking. That was the deal, and Vogel made sure we respected it. Where else could we play anymore? The Collinses had thirteen kids, four of whom slept in their spidery unfinished basement. Our only other option until the caddy shack opened in May was Tim Keough's, and his mom had just told him it was other parents' turn, hint hint, to host us. As far as my own basement went, I couldn't even mention the p-word at home, let alone invite people over to play it. As far as getting stoned was concerned, it would've been too easy for Vogel's old man to smell it, even *if* we'd had something to toke. Pot was more for listening to music, anyway. When Figueroa backed out of the driveway, he was straight and stone sober.

We all were. And by 12:15 we were ready to call it a night. We'd agreed on a cutoff, in fact, six hands in advance. Pat and John Collins and I were all up, Keough was roughly even, Figueroa and Vogel were down.

Especially Figueroa, who'd won for the first couple hours. But he started getting weirdly unlucky, playing reckless with bad cards to try and get even, coming in second a lot. You could tell it was starting to get to him. The closest I could reckon was that by midnight he was at least seventy bucks in the red. He himself wasn't saying.

"It's been real," said Keough. "It's been nice. Just wasn't real nice."

"Oh, but it was," said Pat Collins.

"Share Four," Figueroa said, shuffling. "One last hand."

"Played it five hands ago," John Collins told him. It was one of the few times we'd heard those crazy freckled twins kind of agree with each other, at least about poker or girls.

"Winners don't walk from the table, man," Figueroa said, more insistent.

"What's this, Señor Hoyle?" said Pat. "One of your famous according-to's?"

He was apparently going to let that slide, either because Pat didn't roll his r's or say "Señor Figueroa," or because Mike understood if you threw a punch at one Collins you had to take both of them on. He just said, "They don't, man."

Vogel scooped his hands, tapped his watch. It was closing time.

"They *never* walk?" I said. "So the game lasts forever?"

"No, Duh," said Figueroa, staring at me. "That's not what I'm saying."

"So, what? That we play till everyone's got exactly what he came with?"

Even though the Collinses were mocking him and Vogel was reminding him his old man wanted us out of there, Figueroa stared hardest at me—like he wanted *me* to get killed in a head-on, and maybe a head-on with him. I looked back to say, *So what're you gonna do about it?* It was go time, I thought. Just as well. I might win, I might lose, but so be it. When he didn't say anything else, though, I started dropping bottles and cans into the black plastic garbage bag Vogel snapped open.

"You know Mikey's problem?" said Keough, holding his thumb and index finger up by his ear, then pinching them together. "He's got this very small particle of brain lodged in his skull."

Figueroa anted two quarters, started dealing six hands. "Don't be scared now."

There was nothing else we could think of to say. Except for me, I think everyone sort of felt sorry for him.

"Three bump limit," he said, watching more quarters splash in. "Two bucks a bump after fifth street."

"One last hand," Keough said, "and so now he's explaining the rules?"

Figueroa said, "Sorry, bro. Just making sure."

When I sat back down, he looked across the table at me. We'd never been fond of each other, even before he took Laurie to the dance, this together with the fact that I was sitting on a goodly fraction of his bankroll. Also, I guess, with the fact that his parents had bought him the Impala—a four-door, granted, but black with a red interior, including the make-out-special front bench—and I was still driving my dad's company Olds 88, weekends only, assuming Ellen wasn't home from Barnard and hadn't already called dibs. Our slightly less fuddy-duddy wheels, Gramma's beater Bel Air, had died on Thanksgiving morning, and we couldn't replace it until my dad got his bonus. Insurance didn't cover blown gaskets.

"Mikey loans me some gum after lunch," Keough said, "starts explaining to me how to chew it."

"Said there'd be a chewing quiz Monday morning," John Collins added.

"Who's light?" said Figueroa. He wasn't real tall, but he was dark and what most chicks would call handsome, not to mention spoiled and rich. I'd never seen his house, but his old man imported bananas or guavas or something. He didn't take AP classes or try out for varsity teams. He played clarinet in the orchestra and swam relays for some "aquatic society" halfway to Aurora. Though I couldn't really say I was shocked that Laurie went out with him. It was my own goddamn fault for not asking her myself, especially after Linda had to move. Because it wasn't like Laurie had come out and told me she wanted us to stay just old friends from St. Joan. The other thing was, I'd been writing letters to Linda that whole month before Homecoming and getting exactly one back, with not much to say about *us*. It was mostly about how "mind-bending" James Joyce was, followed the next day by a postcard with Marilyn Monroe in a one-piece reading *Ulysses* while riding a merry-go-round. Whatever a bombshell in a bathing suit reading a banned novel was supposed to mean, with a very pale pink lipstick kiss on the other side, with no other words but my name and address, it pretty much had to be good, even without knowing Linda. Even if the bombshell was dead. (Even more amazing was that the Post Office even delivered it, or that Gramma or my mom didn't intercept it between our mailbox and the kitchen.) So another reason to get my own car was, I could cruise down to Memphis and see her. I should also read the novel, of course. The Book Nook didn't carry it, but I'd heard the Kroch's & Brentano's in Oak Brook always had one in stock. It was supposed to be about Jews, Jesuits, and prostitutes in Dublin, with the dirty parts almost impossible to understand, not really mind-bending in the sense of psychedelic or stoned.

I tossed in my ante and thumbed up the corners of my hole cards: the two scarlet treys. Figueroa turned over the seven of clubs and pushed it to the center of the table. He'd once again chosen this new form of stud called Share Four, in which nobody got their own board cards. Instead, you turned over four "community" cards, one each for streets three through six; seventh was still your third hole card, still dealt down and dirty. He and Vogel both liked it because they said it played faster:

fewer cards to deal, more hands per hour, so the best players could win the most money. Nothing to memorize either, said Vogel, as if giving up an edge you'd worked years to hone was a plus. If you didn't burn cards between streets, up to sixteen people could play at a time, though of course no one's table was big enough. Share Four hadn't even been invented when *The Education* came out a few years ago, so I didn't have much of a feel for it yet. On my own deals I always called jacks-or-better or straight seven-stud.

Both Collinses checked. Vogel, yawning hugely enough to scorch my right ear with his putrid strep-peroni breath, pushed out a dollar. I told him to try Listerine, and he told me to try some myself.

"Try some Dentyne," said Pat Collins, pretending to give me a piece. "Just fold it over and work it back between your molars, like this," he said, helpfully demonstrating.

After Keough and I called the dollar, Figueroa said, "Let's try a quick kick."

One yawn led to another as we tossed in George Washingtons clockwise. For good measure, Pat Collins farted.

The next card was an eight, also of clubs. Vogel bet two, I called, Figueroa bumped it again. The Collinses folded, put on their letterman jackets and headed upstairs. Vogel, always the gracious host, nodded goodbye for the rest of us. As I tossed in my money with the measly treys and no draw, I knew old Herb O. would be twirling around in his grave.

Figueroa said, "Love to see it."

"Then I guess you'll love paying to see these," I said. Because of the mood he was in, it would be almost impossible to bluff him, so I really had my head up my ass.

"Got that right," he said.

Our hard and fast rule was, you could go into your pocket in limit games, but you couldn't go light. When Vogel reminded us of this, Figueroa didn't say anything. He simply flipped the next card—my trey, but of clubs—and brought out his wallet.

"Check to the flushes," said Keough.

Vogel pushed out eight quarters.

"I see your two dollars," I said, "that in all things God may be glorified."

Figueroa was still fishing around in his wallet. He finally pulled out what looked like a dirty gray cigarette filter he'd stepped on and saved for some reason. He unfolded it slowly and tenderly, laid it on top of the pot and began taking change. It was a wrinkled-up twenty. "Kick it two dollars," he said. He must've kept it folded so tightly to discourage himself from spending or losing it. Oops.

As soon as Vogel called, Keough folded. "Take this here pot," he said, to no one in particular, "and buy yourself a hot pork injection."

"That'd be kinda hard," Figueroa said, laughing.

"Harder the better," said Keough, pocketing what was left of his wad.

Figueroa seemed dazed for a moment as he looked across the table at me. As I watched him refocus, I realized I still had zero idea if he knew how I felt about Laurie. The good thing was, he never talked about her or their dates, at least not when I was around. "You'd learn to love it," I said. "Turn the card."

And he did: 4 of clubs.

"All blue," Vogel said, and Figueroa said, "This is true." They were trying so hard to look unexcited, you could tell that they both loved the board: the 7-8-3-4 of clubs. (When Vogel had a boner for his hand, he sometimes looked like he was mad at it, or acted real bored. Figueroa was harder to read, mainly because this was only the second time I'd played with him. He was also just spooky.) I had them both on a flush, though I sensed Figueroa's was bigger.

Vogel and I checked, Figueroa bet, and we called him. With the obvious flushes out there, including a straight flush, a full house was the least I'd be needing. Even with ten outs (three 7s, three 8s, one trey and three 4s) I might be drawing dead, exactly the kind of spot Yardley said only simpletons played themselves into. But something about Figueroa's attitude—everything about it, in fact—made me want to keep chasing. There was also the car thing. Carrying doubles as an A-jock last spring and summer, I'd banked almost eight hundred bucks, till my dad had announced in late August every dime of it was "earmarked" for college. He'd trapped me into saving the maximum, sort of hinting I could spend half of it on a car, then claimed he'd been saying "We'll see" all along. "It's all about priorities, buddy," meaning, in his case, Ellen's room and board in New York, which her scholarship didn't quite cover. Landing an Evans next year *might* dis-earmark enough of it to make a down payment, assuming he'd cosign the note. In the meantime I was basically carless. If I'd won more at poker, of course, I could've bought something decent by now, but my results had been spiking like a lie detector graph since I'd gotten my license in March—trips over trips, queen-high straights losing to king-highs, people spiking miracle cards on the river. Though since Linda had moved down to Memphis, who was I gonna take out anyway in my nonexistent fucking jalopy?

"Deal," Vogel said. "Low and slow."

"Down and dirty," said Figueroa, carefully tossing our last cards face down. I could tell he was nervous. We all were.

My card, of course, was the trey of spades. When we were all through betting the pot was seventy-six dollars and seventy-five cents. Vogel showed down eights full of sevens, Figueroa an ace-high flush. I'd been drawing dead to the trey—to one perfect card. But even if Figueroa had showed us the 5 and 6 of clubs, beating my quads with a freaky straight flush, it would've made pretty much the same difference. Not to me, of course, but to him.

The news got way worse when Vogel called back a half hour later. The Lisle and Naperville cops wanted to speak with us, and so did Figueroa's old man. The cops now had everyone's name and address and would be knocking on my door any minute. I was cringing at the thought of that horror show when Vogel said, "The driver of the truck might die too."

"Oh, Jesus. I forgot about him."

"Yeah, they just laid that one on my folks. To boot, as they say."

As I waited for Vogel to say something else, I imagined sitting way up in the cab of that semi, downshifting and braking like a madman, with the Impala whipping through the four-way in super slow motion, right at you. Trying to stop an eighteen-wheeler weighing however many tons would be like grabbing for tree roots and digging your heels in to slow down your house in a landslide. I couldn't help picturing my parents' faces, arriving home with the groceries and seeing a squad car in the driveway. My dad will be relieved to find out we weren't drinking, I guess, but he'll lose it when he hears what we *were* doing. Gramma will shake her droopy chin to show the cops how mortified she is: how did my sweet lit-tle lamb become such a terrible person? A suspect!

Because I'd already seen it, I told my mom we were going to see *Cool Hand Luke* last night, also because Paul Newman was her favorite star. My new story would have to be that Vogel changed his mind, since I could hardly say we couldn't get a ride or afford $1.20. My dad or the cops might make me give back what I won, though to whom was I supposed to be giving it? Even if I said I broke even, it was still a safe bet I'd be grounded from the car for a month, and after that from driving to anyone's house whose parents might let us play cards. Either way, I decided I should change from my sweatshirt to a blue button-down shirt with a navy V-neck sweater, to look "good" for the cops. And to part my hair on the side, brush it back.

Vogel meanwhile was telling me the wake would be Tuesday at Friedrich Funeral Home in downtown Naperville. "Closed coffin, obviously."

"Prolly not much left for the undertaker to put in a suit," I said.

"Yeah, that'd be quite the undertaking—sorry. Bad joke."

"I served at plenty of funerals back in the day, but this'll be the first time I know the guy inside the box."

"What's so weird is, I never got to actually know him."

"Me neither," I said.

"Just the two times he played in our game, plus being in Trig with him. Guy would *not* share his homework. Mr. Szorc's gonna crap when he hears about it."

"Just before we get in our cars, he says, 'Later, ladies,' meaning me and Keough. Not being a dick or anything, just like, 'I'm cool with losing that much. Get you next time.'"

"So like, 'Nice game, gentlemen'?"

"Almost," I said. "I just don't think he was driving with his panties in a twist."

"So maybe this truck driver's strung out on bennies or something."

"Who knows."

I knew Vogel knew about Figueroa and Laurie, but neither of us brought up the subject. The whole time we were on the phone, I kept waiting for him to say, "And yeah, Duh, it *is* a bit soon to be asking her out." What I wanted to ask him was, if they were still going out, why was Figueroa with us on a date night? Plus, if they were going steady, I'd know it. His ring wrapped with yarn would be on her finger, or hung from a necklace, which I'd easily notice while sitting a knight-move behind her in English. I also wanted to ask Vogel if a girl went to the wake or the funeral if her Homecoming date bought the farm six weeks later. Would she wear a black veil, Jackie Kennedy-style? I should probably call New York and ask Ellen.

"Remember that twenty?" said Vogel.

"Got it right here in my hand." IN GOD WE TRUST, it read, on a banner floating above what was obviously the White House. Right below it, in case there was any confusion, a smaller banner told you, THE WHITE HOUSE. And whoever did the etching of the Mint was pretty damn good at his job. So maybe Figueroa had invited old Laurie to look at *his* etchings, and that was why she broke up with him. Or he asked her to play heads-up strip poker. Share Four, of course, to get her clothes off her faster. Maroon knee-socks first.

"Just like, don't spend it," said Vogel.

I straightened it out, turned it over. Andrew Jackson stared back through the wrinkles and creases. The rectangular folds were smaller and sharper around his face, almost disappearing as they got near the edges. In 1806, when he was a senator, he killed a guy in a duel for insulting his wife, Rachel, and for reneging on some poker or horse-racing bet. The guy shot first and hit Jackson in the chest, but Jackson managed to stay on his feet and shoot the guy in the groin, on purpose, so his death would be slower and more excruciating. The guy's only revenge was that his lead ball stayed in Jackson's chest throughout both his terms in the White House. Even the Surgeon General was afraid to remove it because it was lodged too close to the president's heart. He eventually died of lead poisoning, but not till 1845, when he was seventy-eight, which was like a *hundred* and seventy-eight in those days. Tom Cziesla told me all this while we were looping last summer. "Gotta smart, huh?" he said about the groin shot. "Talk about a low blow." When I told him I doubted a senator and future president would do that, he said, "Yeah? Look it up." I tried to, of course, but it wasn't in *Profiles in Courage* or any encyclopedia. Even if I found the right book or article, how could the author be sure where Jackson was aiming, or why?

"Because you couldn't've played that hand too much

worse," Vogel said.

I finally laughed, pretty hard. "I cannot disagree."

"But he dealt them cards himself, man. Shuffled 'em, forced us to play 'em."

"I know," I said, calming down. I didn't want to be disrespectful.

"Then you gotta go hit your miracle card, so fuck me."

"Sorry, man," I said, though I wasn't, and of course Vogel knew that. With the receiver wedged between my ear bone and shoulder, I was flipping the bill from its gray to its green side and back, snapping the edges to flatten it out.

"Least you got enough now for a beater," said Vogel, "like that Merc they got parked down at Smitty's."

"Not quite, but getting there. The trey kinda helped."

"Nah, ya *think?*"

I was actually thinking about good and bad timing, but also what I'd say to the cops. I hoped they wouldn't ask me who'd lost, who'd won, or how much. If I admitted netting a hundred and forty my dad would make me put my whole roll in the bank, so I could basically kiss it goodbye. But I doubted who won would be the issue for the cops or the coroner, or for anyone else but my dad.

"If he's driving after curfew," I said, "ain't that on *his* folks, not yours?"

"That's what we're gonna find out. My dad has to pay this retainer or something."

"Everybody but you was driving after curfew. They gonna suspend *all* our licenses?"

"Sorry, man," said Vogel.

"So I guess it's fuck *me* then."

"I guess."

When we finally stopped moaning about how tough *our* luck was, Vogel said, "Just a couple guys trying to outguess the light in that slush. You know, man? Just—*totaled*."

"Just bad timing," I said. "We clear out one hand sooner, truck's still down in Romeoville when Figueroa gets to the four-way." What I'd also realized but didn't say out loud was that timing was pretty much why I'd never asked Laurie out. It was why I got picked up by Linda that night, why old Miss Moore didn't turn in my detention, and why she wrote me up in the first place. Plus the motorcade's gotta go past the book depository? Three hundred million blind sperm blast up the tube, wriggling and tumbling and crashing into each other, but only one pierces the ovum? C'mon. Timing was why anything big ever happened, not to mention all the huge things that didn't. Yet I couldn't shake the feeling that Figueroa *also* died because I wanted him to. It wasn't just two random vectors, or who had the green or the yellow.

"Just fuckin' unlucky," said Vogel. "Least he didn't suffer, thank God."

"Yeah, prolly not. But does God make him play that last hand? I don't think so. The poker gods, maybe."

"So now you're saying you don't even believe—"

"I'm saying he takes one extra second, or one second less, before calling or betting—any of us do. Any hand, any street. Or he shuffles my trey one card over." I heard our back door banging open downstairs. My little brother Kevin yelled something about eggnog, and my dad reminded everyone to carry in a bag from the trunk. "Gotta go," I told Vogel. "My folks just got home, but no cops yet."

"I gotta go too. Gotta keep our line open, in case there's *more* heinous news."

"Good luck to your dad with the coroner."

"Yeah, and God help you with yours, Mr. Atheist."

"Just digging through his wallet to find that last twenty." I turned Jackson's face right side up. "That's all I'm saying," I said.

Acknowledgments

"Picasso" originally appeared in *TriQuarterly*, "Detention" in *Fifth Wednesday*, and "Romeoville" in *Chicago Tribune: Printers Row*.

About the Author

James McManus has been called "poker's Shakespeare." He is the *New York Times*-bestselling author of *Positively Fifth Street* and *Cowboys Full: The Story of Poker*, and eight other books. His work has appeared in *The New Yorker, The New York Times, Harper's, The Believer, Paris Review, Esquire*, and in *Best American* anthologies of poetry, sports writing, science and nature, and magazine writing. He has received the Carl Sandburg Award for Fiction, the Peter Lisagor Award for Sports Journalism, as well as fellowships from the Guggenheim and Rockefeller foundations. He teaches at The School of the Art Institute of Chicago.

BOA Editions, Ltd. American Reader Series

No. 1 *Christmas at the Four Corners of the Earth*
Prose by Blaise Cendrars
Translated by Bertrand Mathieu

No. 2 *Pig Notes & Dumb Music: Prose on Poetry*
By William Heyen

No. 3 *After-Images: Autobiographical Sketches*
By W. D. Snodgrass

No. 4 *Walking Light: Memoirs and Essays on Poetry*
By Stephen Dunn

No. 5 *To Sound Like Yourself: Essays on Poetry*
By W. D. Snodgrass

No. 6 *You Alone Are Real to Me: Remembering Rainer Maria Rilke*
By Lou Andreas-Salomé

No. 7 *Breaking the Alabaster Jar: Conversations with Li-Young Lee*
Edited by Earl G. Ingersoll

No. 8 *I Carry A Hammer In My Pocket For Occasions Such As These*
By Anthony Tognazzini

No. 9 *Unlucky Lucky Days*
By Daniel Grandbois

No. 10 *Glass Grapes and Other Stories*
By Martha Ronk

No. 11 *Meat Eaters & Plant Eaters*
By Jessica Treat

No. 12 *On the Winding Stair*
By Joanna Howard

No. 13 *Cradle Book*
By Craig Morgan Teicher

No. 14 *In the Time of the Girls*
By Anne Germanacos

No. 15 *This New and Poisonous Air*
By Adam McOmber

No. 16 *To Assume a Pleasing Shape*
By Joseph Salvatore

No. 17 *The Innocent Party*
By Aimee Parkison

No. 18 *Passwords Primeval: 20 American Poets in Their Own Words*
Interviews by Tony Leuzzi

No. 19 *The Era of Not Quite*
By Douglas Watson

No. 20 *The Winged Seed: A Remembrance*
By Li-Young Lee

No. 21 *Jewelry Box: A Collection of Histories*
By Aurelie Sheehan

No. 22 *The Tao of Humiliation*
By Lee Upton

No. 23 *Bridge*
By Robert Thomas

No. 24 *Reptile House*
By Robin McLean

No. 25 *The Education of a Poker Player*
James McManus

Colophon

BOA Editions, Ltd., a not-for-profit publisher of poetry and other literary works, fosters readership and appreciation of contemporary literature. By identifying, cultivating, and publishing both new and established poets and selecting authors of unique literary talent, BOA brings high-quality literature to the public. Support for this effort comes from the sale of its publications, grant funding, and private donations.

The publication of this book is made possible, in part, by the special support of the following individuals:

Anonymous x 2
Armbruster Family Foundation
Dr. James & Ann Burk, *in memory of Dr. John Hoey*
Gwen & Gary Conners
Jenna & Steve Fisher
Gouvernet Arts Fund
Michael Hall
Boo Poulin
Deborah Ronnen & Sherman Levey
Steven O. Russell & Phyllis Rifkin-Russell
Sue S. Stewart, *in memory of Stephen L. Raymond*
Dan & Nan Westervelt,
in honor of Whitman, Max & Kane Conners